
⋆

"Sister Barbara was murdered," Mother Celeste said. "All these years I've hidden the truth. All my life I've been a coward."

"How was she murdered?"

"She was poisoned. Or given drugs. I don't know which."

"Who did it?"

"The name of the murderer is not important. God knows who did it, and I know, and Sister Barbara in heaven knows. The important thing is, I never had the courage to tell the murderer I knew what happened. I never made sure the murderer went to confession. And now it's too late. I'm too weak. That's what I asked you to come down here for. To do what I'm too weak to do."

⋆

D0449470

sister Barbara was puzzled too," Mother Celeste
said. "All these worries aside, is she truly willing
to—? We have a queue."

"How long can we stand it?"

She was puzzled. "Oh, yes, unless I don't know
what—"

"Why didn't I—"

"The nuns of the mind, this is my imagination, God
knows, who did it, and I know, and Sister Barbara
has been warned. The important thing is, I haven't
had the courage to tell the remaining. I know what
he need. I have made sure the mind whatever it
continues. Anyhow he has left me. I'm too weak.
That's where she told you to come when you've been in To
do what I want to want to do."

"I don't see why not," said Sister R. "Unless you realize
Sister Barbara is totally that now inundated at
otherwise so de—

"He will know, review—

"Well, come back, go back," she's sister too—"
with more to believe.

Murder at St. Adelaide's

Gerelyn Hollingsworth

WORLDWIDE.

TORONTO • NEW YORK • LONDON
AMSTERDAM • PARIS • SYDNEY • HAMBURG
STOCKHOLM • ATHENS • TOKYO • MILAN
MADRID • WARSAW • BUDAPEST • AUCKLAND

MURDER AT ST. ADELAIDE'S

A Worldwide Mystery/November 1997

First published by St. Martin's Press, Incorporated.

ISBN 0-373-26255-8

Printed In U.S.A.

For Jerry and Nicholas

ONE

THREE MESSAGES.

"Frances, this is Sharon. I'm at the motherhouse. Please call me as soon as you can. It's quarter to twelve. Thank you."

Sister Sharon Bieralski had been one of my teachers at St. Adelaide's Academy, and over the years we had remained friends. We talked on the phone every month or so. She would call to tell me when one of the old nuns died, or one of my former classmates got a divorce. Once or twice a year we went out to dinner.

"Frances, it's Sharon again. It's three o'clock. Please call me as soon as possible. It's very important. Thank you."

Since I never went to funerals or alumnae reunions or anything else at St. Adelaide's, Sharon was never urgent.

"Frances, it's me again. It's nine o'clock. Call no matter how late you get in."

She answered on the first ring. She must have been sitting in the motherhouse office. "Frances, thank God."

"What's wrong?"

"Mother Celeste is dying."

Mother Celeste was about a hundred, so I wasn't surprised. "What's wrong with her?"

"The doctor says her body is just worn out. She's so old, her body is just dying by inches. They had to take out eighteen inches of bowel last week."

"Is she in pain?"

"We have medication for her. Most of the time she doesn't want it. She wants to be clear."

I wondered what this had to do with me. "Does she know she's dying?"

"Oh, yes. She insists the doctor tell her everything."

"How long does she have left?"

"It could be any day now. Any minute. The doctor just doesn't know."

"Well, I'm sorry to hear it. What are *you* doing down there?" Sharon was principal of the Adelaides' school here in Kansas City. She usually avoided the mother-house.

"My heart gave a little flutter in May, and the doctor said I had to spend the summer down here in the infirmary."

"You had a heart attack?"

"Not an official heart attack. Just an intimation of mortality. Frances, Mother wants to see you."

"Me?" Mother Celeste couldn't stand me. She hadn't liked me when I was in school, and she thought it was a disgrace that a St. Adelaide's girl had become a private investigator. When my dad died and I took over the agency, she criticized me to everyone. When a case I was involved with a couple of years ago made the newspaper in Kansas City, Sharon wanted to reprint the story in the *Alumnae Bulletin*, but Mother Celeste wouldn't let her. "Why would she want to see me?"

"She won't tell me. But she's obsessed with the idea of talking to you before she dies. She keeps telling me to get you down here. Maybe she's going to change your English grade."

I had suffered through Mother Celeste's famous English composition class my senior year. She always wrote the same thing on my papers: "Good, but not your best." She had given me a *C* as my final grade, keeping me out of the honor society.

Braddock, Kansas, is sixty miles south of Kansas City. I drove down the old highway. In my school days it had been the main route, but now the interstate had taken its traffic and left it deserted. The farms where my dad and I used to stop to get fresh eggs and tomatoes no longer had hand-lettered signs at their gates. The speed traps in the small towns along the way were no more. The Dairy Queens were boarded up.

I missed the exit. I pulled into a little gas station, a perfectly preserved artifact of the thirties. Since I was asking and not buying, I got out of my car and went inside.

The man behind the desk stared at me. Then he did an exaggerated double take. He stood up and came around the desk to shake hands with me. "Frances Finn? Unbelievable!"

"Hello, Jack." Jack Braddock and I were the same age. When I was a student at St. Adelaide's, he was going to Braddock High. He and his friends used to drive around the St. Ad's campus at night, honking, squealing brakes, ringing the old convent bell, driving the nuns nuts.

"You look the same as ever," he said.

"So do you." Gorgeous still. But why is this scion of the town's second richest family sitting out here in a miserable little gas station on an abandoned highway? Why are his hands clean at eleven o'clock?

St. Adelaide's girls didn't date Braddock High boys, but we knew them. When they yelled up at our dorm windows late at night, we recognized their voices. Sometimes we found ourselves sitting with them in the booths in Harley's Drugstore. Jack Braddock and I had taken walks together on a few Sunday afternoons when we were seniors.

"I guess I shouldn't be surprised," Jack said. "Everybody comes back sooner or later. I assume you're on your way to St. Ad's?"

"If I can find it. What happened to the exit?"

"Where the overpass was, a mile and a half back? That's where the old exit used to be. But just stay on this road. This road goes right into town now. From the east." He walked outside with me. "Nice car."

"Thank you."

"You down here to say good-bye to Mother Celeste?" Jack Braddock was related to Mother Celeste. He used to serve mass occasionally in the convent chapel.

"Yes."

"She's in bad shape."

"That's what I hear."

"Well, she's had a long life. It runs in the family. We're long-lived." He waved as I drove away.

The back gate to St. Adelaide's was open, and I drove past the chaplain's house and up to the old convent. Sharon was sitting on the porch. She got up and ran down the walk. She pulled me out of the car and gave me a hug. She wasn't moving like a person who had had a heart attack.

Sharon Bieralski was in her fifties. She was dark-eyed, small and graceful, always well-groomed. She had been beautiful in the old Adelaide habit, and she had made the transition to ordinary clothes with ease. Today she was wearing navy slacks and a blue-and-white-striped blouse.

We walked inside arm in arm. It was dark and cool

in the old convent even though the 1895 building was not air-conditioned. Waves of the past washed over me, and I leaned against the carved banister to inhale the fragrance of St. Adelaide's.

"I thought you'd like to stay in your old room," Sharon said.

We went up the stairs to the third floor. The building was empty, Sharon told me, except for Sister Zita who still lived in the student infirmary on the first floor. The nuns had closed St. Adelaide's Academy in the late seventies. Catholic girls from farms and small towns who used to board at convent schools had begun to stay home then and attend their local public high schools.

My room looked the same as ever. The window was open, and Sharon and I climbed out onto the fire escape. It had been for this high perch that I chose this room at the beginning of my sophomore year and stayed in it until I graduated. Here was a place to hide and smoke and ditch study hall and spy on the novices at their evening recreation. Through the branches of a century-old cedar tree I could see all of St. Adelaide's. Below was the lilac field where the novices played softball. To the left was the motherhouse with the gardens and the barnyard behind it. To the right was the long drive curving down past the grotto and the pergola to the main gate. In the distance, at the south end of the campus, was the nuns' graveyard.

"How is Mother Celeste?"

"She's good today. I told her you were driving down this morning. She's happy about that."

"What does she want with me?"

"She won't tell me. She's so stubborn. The same as ever. Be prepared."

We climbed back inside. The narrow bed had a white

cover on it embroidered in the center with a yellow crown above a blue *A*, the needlework of a long-ago novice, maybe Mother Celeste.

"Where is she?"

"In the infirmary. She's with her nephew now. They play bridge every morning."

"Bridge?"

"Honeymoon. He leaves at noon, and she has dinner. She doesn't really eat anymore. Then I help her brush her teeth. Then she rests. She wants to see you at three. She's at her best then, pain-wise." Sharon looked at her watch. "Will you come with me to the refectory? I can think of several nuns who would love to see you."

"No, thanks. I think I'll go uptown. Is Harley's still there? Join me in a B.L.T.?"

"I'd love to, but I'm supposed to be eating a special heart diet. Sister Jeanette would be annoyed if I didn't turn up at dinner."

"Jeanette's alive? I thought she died years ago. Didn't she have cancer?"

"She beat it. She refused chemotherapy, and got better on her own. Prayer. I don't know what we'd do without her. She's the only nurse left in the community. We've got forty nuns left, and twenty of them are in the infirmary. Jeanette takes care of all of them." Sharon went out to the hall. "Call me when you get back from town. I think the house phone over here still works. I'll be in the office."

Sharon left, and I opened my suitcase. I hung my clothes in the little Victorian wardrobe that used to hold my school uniforms. The oval mirror on the door distorted my face in the same old way. I looked young and innocent on the left side, and old and cynical on the right side.

I looked out the window. Sharon was crossing the campus. She felt me watching her and turned to wave. I was worried about her. Besides being principal of the Adelaides' school in Kansas City—the only one that brought in any money to the community anymore—Sharon was assistant superior. I knew she felt responsible for the old nuns and the old buildings. Mother Celeste was dying, and the order was dying, and the deathbed duties were Sharon's.

I heard a familiar sound. A nun was coming down the hall, rosary beads clacking at her side. It could be only one person, since only one person still wore the old habit. "Sister Zita!"

"Hello, Frances." Zita was too shy to hug me or shake hands or anything like that. She had been waiting downstairs for Sharon to leave so she could come up and talk to me. Zita avoided the other nuns, particularly important ones like Sharon.

Zita had been the academy infirmarian when I was in school. She wasn't a nurse like Sister Jeanette, just a woman who had been a servant in a doctor's house before entering the convent. She had been a late vocation, in her thirties when she entered. She was in her late sixties now.

Zita would have been a lay sister in the days when convents had lay sisters. She never went to prayers or recreation or meals in the refectory or anything else with the other nuns. She kept to the barnyard, the laundry, the girls' infirmary where she lived, and the chaplain's house where she served and cleaned. She always knew all the gossip. I used to pump her for information about the nuns and then amaze my teachers with what I knew.

"What does Mother Celeste want with you?" Zita asked. "Is she consulting you professionally?"

Trust Zita to put it into words. Was Mother Celeste going to ask me to investigate something? Was she going to have me look into the background of a prospective postulant? Were there such things as postulants anymore? "That's what I've been wondering. I figured you'd know."

"They don't tell me anything." Zita put my pajamas and underwear into a drawer. She arranged my toiletries and cosmetics on the dresser. "What's new with you? I saw the thing about you in the paper."

We talked as easily as if it were yesterday that I last sat with her in the infirmary, malingering, ditching mass or gym or a test. Zita told me that she had heard from the kitchen sisters that Mother Celeste had not eaten for four days. "It won't be long now."

The Angelus bell began to ring. Zita said, "I've got to take care of Father's dinner. I'll see you later. You can use the shower down in the infirmary. There's no hot water up here. And here's a key to the front door."

TWO

I WALKED uptown. Many people in Braddock, not just the nuns, ate dinner at noon. The smell of substantial meals cooking came from the windows of the little houses out by St. Ad's.

As I got closer to the town square, the bungalows gave way to large Victorian houses. They were well maintained. Their gingerbread was painted, and their porches were decorated with wicker furniture and ferns. Braddock Brothers Funeral Home, the second biggest house in town, gleamed in the sun, yellow and blue and gray.

I reached the square. The Union Hotel on the north side had been restored and had an antique shop and a restaurant on the first floor. The Southern Hotel looked as shabby as ever. The Bank of Braddock looked the same as when the Dalton boys robbed it. The old one-cell stone jail still leaned against the movie theater. The feed store and the John Deere showroom were next. I stuck my head in the open door of the feed store to get the smell.

Harley's was on the west side of the square. I went inside and inhaled another delicious fragrance, small town drugstore. I took a comic book from the rack and sat at the counter. I felt like I was sixteen again. I wasn't surprised to hear Jack Braddock's voice. "We meet again."

He sat on the stool next to mine and ordered a cheese-burger. I asked for a B.L.T. and a limeade. The counterwoman made everything from scratch. She and Jack knew each other and everyone in the booths. Everyone talked to everyone else. Jack pointed out a man in the last booth. "Remember that guy? He was a junior when we were seniors? Drove a fifty-five Buick?"

I was sitting at a drugstore counter on the town square in Braddock, Kansas, with an old not-exactly flame but maybe flicker who in middle age still identified people by the cars they drove in high school. Just an hour from my ordinary life was this Andy Hardy place. "I don't think I remember him. I remember *your* car though."

"Black Beauty."

"Was that its name?"

"*Her* name. My baby. I wish I had her now. My wife made me sell her. After we got divorced, I tried to get her back. Black Beauty, not my wife. You married?"

"No."

"I can't get over how you look, Frances. The same as ever."

"I'd forgotten how beautiful Braddock was."

"Braddock the town or Braddock the boy?"

"The funeral home looks like it should be on the cover of *Architectural Digest*."

"Thanks. I painted it. My brother thought the yellow would be too loud, but I talked him into it."

"It's beautiful."

"I'd like for you to see the inside. I did that, too."

We reminisced about high school days while we ate our lunch. Jack gave me a ride back to St. Ad's on his way back out to the filling station.

Someone had been in my room while I was uptown. Sister Zita. She had put a little electric fan on the desk and towels and a bar of soap on the bed. A vase of flowers was on the nightstand.

I decided to take a shower and change before seeing Mother Celeste. I put on my robe and slippers and went down to the infirmary. The girls' infirmary consisted of two bedrooms. Zita slept in the second one. The first one had been for students. The two narrow beds in it were made. I went into the tiny bathroom behind the students' room and took a shower.

I went back upstairs to dress. I had a suit with me, but it was too hot for that, and I wasn't sure I was here on business. I put on slacks and a silk blouse, sandals, jewelry. I wanted to look successful so Mother Celeste would apologize for criticizing my choice of careers.

I dialed the convent office on the house phone. The phone was another artifact from the past, a candlestick model that was housed in a little cupboard in the wall.

Sharon answered. "Come on over," she said. "I'll meet you in front."

I crossed the campus to the motherhouse. Sharon was leaning against the base of the statue of St. Adelaide. This was the traditional meeting place at St. Ad's. Queen Adelaide, the patron of the order, stood facing west, her arms extended in welcome. She was in sandals too, and her feet were shiny from generations of academy girls and nuns rubbing them for luck as they passed. "Peacemaker of Europe" was carved on the front of the base; on the back was carved, "She never forgot a kindness, nor ever remembered an injury." I rubbed her foot.

"You ready?" Sharon asked.

"Is this going to be gruesome?" I was afraid Mother Celeste would look like a skeleton, or smell.

"You're so squeamish. How can a detective be so squeamish?"

We went up the stone steps to the big porch and into

the motherhouse. Sharon led me past the parlors and the office and into the southwest wing. I had never been down this corridor before. In my school days, the academy girls were not allowed to go into the cloistered areas of the convent.

There were several old nuns sitting in a little solarium. I recognized my old chemistry teacher, but she had forgotten her least promising student. This entire wing was the convent infirmary now, Sharon told me. Mother Celeste had the corner room at the end of the hall. The door was open, and we went in.

"Welcome, Frances," Mother Celeste said. She had a mop of white curls, and her famous smile looked the same as ever. She didn't look bad for someone who was dying. She was sitting up in bed, propped against several pillows.

The windows and a door to the porch were open, and the room smelled fresh.

"It's good to see you, Mother," I said. And it was. I felt like a child again. When my dad first brought me to St. Adelaide's, I was thirteen. We sat in a little parlor with Mother Celeste. She was wearing the old habit then, yards of black serge, beautifully draped and pleated, cinctured with a long leather belt. Her freckled face was framed by a white coif and guimpe. Her long, sheer veil hung from her starched headband. She enrolled me in the academy and assured my dad that I would be well taken care of at St. Adelaide's and would love boarding school.

"Thank you for coming, Frances. I know you're very busy." She nodded at Sharon, dismissing her. "Thank you, Sister," she said as Sharon left the room, closing the door behind her.

"Sit down, Frances."

I sat.

"I need your help."

"Yes, Mother."

"Do you remember Sister Barbara?"

"Yes, Mother." Sister Barbara was a young nun who died when I was a sophomore at the academy. I could picture her still, young and beautiful in her coffin, her waxy hands holding her vows. She was a daughter of Peter Ross, the richest man in town. Her younger sister was in my class in school. I remembered every detail of her funeral, the rain, the open grave, her distraught family, the nuns singing "In Paradisum" as they carried her coffin down to the graveyard.

"I'm going to be standing before God in a few days. Did Sister Sharon tell you?"

"Yes, Mother."

"Do you know that a religious superior is held responsible at her judgment, not only for her own failings, but for those of everyone under her?"

"Yes, Mother." A cruel and crazy notion, I thought, but I wouldn't try to change the thinking of an old woman now.

"I can't face God until I take care of something I should have taken care of years ago. I need your help."

"I'll be glad to help you in any way I can."

"Your father was a dear man. I always liked him so much."

My dad liked Mother Celeste, too. When he would come down to St. Ad's to take me home for a weekend or a vacation, he would come an hour or so early to have some time to spend talking to her. I would find him in her office when I got out of my last class.

"Your father was a brave man."

"Yes, Mother."

"I wouldn't want to put you in danger."

"Tell me what I can do for you, Mother."

"Sister Barbara was murdered."

"Murdered? I thought she died of a cerebral hemorrhage."

"That's what I let everyone think. I've hidden the truth all these years."

"Sister Barbara was *murdered?*" The ugly word was out of place in this clean convent room. Murder? I don't do murder. The detective business isn't about murder. At least mine isn't. The cops do murder. Not even my dad did murder. Maybe one murder. I spend my days tracking down the birth parents of adult adoptees. Sometimes I look into the backgrounds of prospective bridegrooms. "How do you know?"

"Because she was wearing her scapular when we found her. If she had committed suicide, she would not have put on her scapular."

"Suicide?" Which was it, murder or suicide?

"Some of the nuns thought Sister Barbara took her own life. She had been sick for months. She had contracted a tropical disease in Guatemala, and some of the nuns thought she was in despair over her health. I let them go on thinking that. I was willing to let them think that rather than risk a scandal. But she didn't kill herself. She had her scapular on. Sister Barbara would not have committed a sacrilege as her last act on earth."

Catholics believed that anyone who died wearing a scapular would be taken from purgatory to heaven by the Virgin Mary on the Saturday after death. It would be a mockery to put a scapular on and then kill yourself.

"Sister Barbara was murdered," Mother Celeste said. "All these years I've hidden the truth. All my life I've been a coward."

"How was she murdered?"

"She was poisoned. Or given drugs. I don't know which."

"Was there an autopsy?"

"No. A cerebral hemorrhage would have been the typical outcome of the disease she had. The virus goes to the brain. The doctor just assumed that's what happened and signed the death certificate without question."

"Who did it?"

Mother Celeste let her head fall back on the pillows. She closed her eyes, and I could see the pain on her face. She said, "The name of the murderer is not important. God knows who did it, and I know, and Sister Barbara in heaven knows. The important thing is, I never had the courage to tell the murderer I knew what happened. I never made sure the murderer went to confession. I kept putting it off. Through cowardice. And now it's too late. I'm too weak. That's what I asked you to come down here for. To do what I'm too weak to do. I know you have courage, Frances. Your father had courage, and I know you do, too. I want Sister Barbara's name cleared. Poor Sister. I want everyone to know that she didn't commit suicide. I can't face my particular judgment until I take care of this. Poor Sister. She was so young. It wasn't bad enough that she was murdered, but her memory in the community is tainted. I know I'll have to spend time in purgatory for this. Will you pray for me, Frances?"

She started crying then. She said, "I'm sorry. I have to rest. I'm sorry. I can't talk anymore. I hope you never know this kind of pain and weakness. I'll tell you what I want you to do tomorrow. You'll stay overnight? Will you come at eleven? My nephew wants to be here when

I talk to you. He'll take care of the financial arrangements."

I left the room. Sharon was in the hall talking to one of the old nuns. She went outside with me. We sat on the bench by the statue of St. Adelaide.

"Well?"

"I'm not sure what she wants me to do. I'm supposed to talk to her again in the morning."

THREE

SHARON WAS under doctor's orders to lie down and rest every afternoon, so she left me. I decided to do a little preliminary research.

I walked down to the graveyard. A stone wall surrounded the nuns' burial place. I opened the iron gate and went in. The three founders of St. Adelaide's were buried on a mound in the center. I climbed the steps and read the familiar inscriptions on their headstones. All three had been born in the 1850s, and all three had died in the 1930s. They were three friends who had decided to break from their old convent in Kentucky. They were Americans, and the German prayers, the German teaching methods, and the German rule which included the requirement that the nuns speak German at all times were too much for them. They came to Kansas in 1894.

I went down the steps and back to the oldest part of the graveyard, to the place where the first members of the new community had been buried. Three nuns, all under twenty, the entire first class of novices, had died in 1897. Tuberculosis, the killer of young nuns, had taken them all. The founders nearly gave up then. They nearly returned to Kentucky. But other postulants entered, and the order began to grow. It was not until Sister Barbara Ross died that another nun under thirty was laid to rest in this place.

Her grave was in the third row. On her stone cross it said: Sister M. Barbara Ross, R.S.A. 1940-1965 R.I.P.

Five more rows had filled up since Sister Barbara's death. Several of my old teachers had died: Sister Roberta, the great convent organist; Sister Vivian, my old dorm prefect; Sister Helen Marie, the beautiful novice mistress; Sister Monica, my old Latin teacher. All were dead.

Had Sister Barbara really been murdered, or was Mother Celeste's mind affected by pain and morphine and old age? If Barbara Ross *had* been murdered, who did it? And why? How was I to investigate such a matter? If Mother Celeste knew who did it, why did she need an investigator? If all she wanted was to get the murderer to go to confession, why didn't she just tell him—or her—herself? Or have the chaplain do it? Or her nephew?

I walked back to the old convent and got in my car. I needed to call my answering machine, and I didn't want to use the convent phone with its innumerable extensions. I called on my car phone and took down the messages. Nothing of importance.

I drove uptown. I parked on the square in front of the *Braddock Herald*, the newspaper published by Sister Barbara Ross's father. I went inside. An ancient printing press was on display in the front window, and on the walls were framed front pages with headlines about Pearl Harbor, Roosevelt's death, Japan's surrender. No one was at the desk. I knocked on the wooden counter, and a woman came out of the back room. It was my old classmate, Pauline Ross.

"Hello, Frances." She wasn't surprised to see me.

"Hello, Pauline."

"Mother Celeste got you down here."

"You knew about it?"

"She had me out there last week. She told me she

was going to try to get you to come down here. She's decided to tell the truth about my sister after all these years, hasn't she? Does she have a note?''

''A note?''

''I always thought Barbara would have left a note. She always wrote wonderful letters. I couldn't believe she'd commit suicide and not leave a note.''

''Your sister committed suicide?''

''Of course. Isn't that what Mother Celeste told you?''

''She didn't really tell me anything. She tried to tell me what she wants with me, but the pain got to her. I'm supposed to talk to her again tomorrow.''

''I think she's going to have you break the news to the nuns. The ones who didn't figure it out for themselves years ago.''

''I always thought your sister died of a cerebral hemorrhage.''

''That's what Mother Celeste put out. It would have been a big scandal back then if a nun committed suicide. Although Barb wasn't the only one. When I was in college, I heard about a nun from a big order who jumped out a window after she flunked her doctoral exams.''

''Why would your sister kill herself?''

''She was miserable in the convent. She wanted to leave from day one. My parents wouldn't let her. Mother Celeste wouldn't let her.''

''Did you know that then?''

''No. I swallowed the b.s. like everyone else. Barb was a saintly little martyr, cut down by a tropical disease in the bloom of youth. But as I got older, I figured it out.''

"Did your parents know? *Do* they know? Are your parents still alive?"

"Very much so. Still live in the old house."

The Ross house was across the street from Braddock Brothers Funeral Home. "The house looks fabulous," I said. "Did Jack Braddock paint it?"

"How did you know that?"

"I'm a detective. Plus, I saw him at Harley's at lunch. He told me he painted the funeral home. Your house looks the same. Better."

"He copied the color scheme from a book on San Francisco houses."

"Did your parents know Barbara killed herself?"

"They pretended not to, but they knew. They had to know. There was a lot of pretense in our family. They hadn't invented the term 'dysfunctional family' when Barbara died, or 'anorexia nervosa' for that matter. Two useful terms that explain what happened to my big sister. I guess that's what Mother Celeste wants you to do. Make everybody face the truth."

"Why would she need me for that? She could do that herself. Or have her nephew do it."

"Eddie Braddock? Why would he do it? He's a moron."

"Why can't *you* do it?"

"I'm not interested in forcing truth on anyone. Least of all my parents. I just hang around here and write the hog and sorghum news. I let the ghosts take care of themselves."

Pauline Ross and I hadn't been particularly close in school, but I had always liked her. She was a day student, and I was a boarder. She used to spend the night in the dorm when we had slumber parties, and I had spent the night at her house a couple of times. I remembered how she behaved when Sister Barbara died. Was murdered. Was she murdered? Pauline sat in the chapel, slumped over with sorrow. On the first day, before the body was brought back to the convent from the funeral home, Pauline sat in the back of the chapel, but for the next two days, while Sister Barbara was laid out, Pauline sat in the front pew by the coffin.

On the day they brought Barbara's body back to the convent, they wheeled the coffin up the aisle and opened it. Pauline and her parents and her brother went up first. Pauline looked down at her dead sister and then opened her mouth as if she were about to scream. Her brother, a priest, put his arm around her, and led her away. She didn't scream, but her mouth stayed open in a silent scream. For the next two days, until the funeral, she sat by the coffin, slumped over.

Early on the morning of the funeral, I watched Pauline from my window. She walked down to the cemetery and stood by the empty grave in the rain. She stared into the hole for an hour. I watched her through my binoculars.

"Pauline," I said, "do you have all the old *Heralds*?"

"Sure. From Volume One, Number One. Bound volumes. You want to read about Barb's death?"

"If that's okay."

"Dad wrote an editorial about her. William Allen White. Remember William Allen White? The editorial about Mary White? In our English book? Dad always thought of himself as another William Allen White." She led me up a narrow staircase to a room upstairs. The walls were lined with shelves holding the bound volumes. There was a table by the window. I could see the town square out the window.

Pauline took a volume off a shelf and put it on the table. "There were stories about Barb on December second and December sixth. The *Herald* came out three times a week then. Dad wrote his editorial about her on Christmas Eve."

"Thanks."

"I'll leave you to it. By the way, are you staying at the convent?"

"In my old room."

"What are you doing for dinner?"

"I thought I might go to Harley's again."

"Eat with me, okay? Talk about old times?"

"Okay. Sure."

"I'll pick you up at six. We'll go to the country club." Pauline went downstairs.

Braddock, Kansas. Thursday, December 2, 1965. Sister Mary Barbara Ross, a Sister of St. Adelaide, died yesterday at the motherhouse. She was twenty-five years old.

Sister Barbara was the daughter of Peter and Winifred Ross, publishers of the *Braddock Herald*. She is survived by her parents, by her twin brother, the Reverend Thomas A. Ross, a priest of the Diocese of East Central Kansas, and by her sister, Pauline Ross, of the family home.

Sister Barbara was a 1957 graduate of St. Adelaide's Academy. She entered the convent on June 16, 1957, and received the habit six months later. She was admitted to temporary profession in 1959, and on December 16, 1962, she pronounced her final vows.

Sister Barbara taught fourth grade at St. George's School in Braddock from 1959 through

1963. In 1963, Sister Barbara, along with Sister Mary Sharon Bieralski, established the Adelaides' first foreign mission, a school for Mayan girls in Guatemala. Sister Barbara contracted an illness in Guatemala which forced her to return to the United States in 1964. She suffered a fatal cerebral accident in her sleep early Wednesday morning.

There will be visitation in the convent chapel today and tomorrow. His Excellency, the Right Reverend Bishop Joseph S. Leet, will celebrate a Requiem Mass in the chapel at 10:00 a.m. on Saturday, December 4. Burial in the convent cemetery will follow. Funeral arrangements are made through Braddock Brothers Funeral Home.

Barbara's obituary was on the front page. There was a picture of her in the old habit. It was her Profession Day picture. There was a wreath of roses on her black-veiled head.

On December sixth, there was a front page story about Sister Barbara's funeral. There was a big picture of the procession. Six nuns, Barbara's profession classmates, were pallbearers. They were followed by the bishop, several priests, several altar boys, Mother Celeste and the council, the Ross family, the nuns, the novices and postulants, and the academy girls. It was a wonderful picture, gloriously sad, of a long line of habits, school uniforms, umbrellas. I knew which sophomore was me, but I was too far back for my face to be clear. Curly-haired Jack Braddock, angelic in cassock and surplice, was a candlebearer.

On December twenty-fourth, Peter Ross's editorial about his daughter ran on the front page.

The twins were born February 10, 1940. Barbara came first. She was followed a few minutes later by her brother Tom. Barbara would always take the lead. Winnie and I always knew that whatever mischief the twins got into had been Barbara's idea. Tommy was her willing follower.

Barbara was quick to learn and eager to teach. When I enlisted in the Navy in 1942, the twins had just turned two. They were talking, speaking a language of their own. By 1944, both twins could read, and Barbara could write. By 1945, Barbara had taught her brother to write, and both of them sent letters to me. In one of those letters, the twins announced that they planned to enter religious life. Barbara was going to be a nun and Tommy was going to be a priest. I have the V-mail copy of that letter before me as I write. The twins decorated it with a picture of Mickey, their bull terrier.

Barbara never wavered in her vocation. Throughout grade school and high school she worked at the *Herald* on weekends and in the summer. She did everything. She took classified ads over the phone, set type, swept the floor. Sometimes she would look up from her work and say, "How will you get along without me, Dad?"

She meant, of course, how would I get the paper out after she entered the convent. But that part was easy. The hard part was going home from work and not having Barbara there to call down to me from her window, not having her there to run down the steps to give me a hug, not having her there at the supper table to argue with about politics, religion, literature, and everything else.

After Barbara entered the novitiate, Winnie and

I would walk out to St. Adelaide's on Sundays to visit her. We missed her terribly, but knowing she was only ten minutes away made it bearable. After our daughter made vows and began teaching, my wife and I would walk over to St. George's at lunch time and watch Barbara at recess with her students, jumping rope, building snowmen, playing kickball. Then came the news from Mother Celeste that our girl would be going to Guatemala. "How will you get along without me, Dad?" Barbara asked.

I knelt beside her in the chapel on the day she received her mission cross. The pain was almost too much to bear. But would I want to deprive the children of the Maya the chance to have Barbara as their teacher? Would I keep my daughter safe in Kansas when she was needed in a Central American jungle?

Barbara sent us pictures from the mission: children with ancient faces, a schoolhouse with a straw roof, herself in a white habit. And then she came back. Our girl was sick with a sickness that had ended her laughter and would end her life.

Now Winnie and I have buried our daughter. Now we walk out to the convent and stand by her grave. Now only the question remains: "How will you get along without me, Dad?"

FOUR

PAULINE DROVE UP the long drive at six, and parked in front of the old convent. The Angelus was ringing from the motherhouse dome. Pauline got out of her car and looked up at my window. She was wearing a white dress. She was tall and handsome, strong-featured, athletic.

I called down to her. "Come up or wait on the porch. I'll be down in two minutes."

She came up. "This place smells exactly the same," she said. She looked out the window. "I used to envy you so much for living here. I used to beg my parents to let me board."

I was still in my robe. I wasn't sure of the dress code at the Braddock Country Club. "What should I wear?" I showed her the two choices in the wardrobe.

"The yellow."

Pauline went out in the hall, and opened the doors of the empty rooms. "Can you see the ghosts?"

"Sure. Trish is sitting there at her desk writing to her boyfriend."

"Mike."

"Playing the Beatles on her record player."

"Ellen and Julie are studying."

"Or ironing uniform blouses."

"When I would come up here after school and you guys would be in your rooms, I would be so jealous."

"I thought you were happy being a day student. No bullshit rules."

"Being a day student at a boarding school is terrible."

"But you had a fabulous house. Your room was like a princess's room. In a tower. Rapunzel. Your canopy bed. All the Raggedy Anns."

We walked down the steps to the second floor. We looked in all the rooms and named the girls who had lived in them. "Remember Hortensia?"

"God, she was always smoking. The whole building reeked of her cigarettes."

"The nuns would accuse her, and she would deny it, but the room would be filled with clouds of blue smoke."

"Gauloises."

We went down to the first floor and looked in the classrooms. The moldings and the fireplace mantels had been removed. "What happened to all the woodwork?" I asked.

"The nuns had a sale a few years ago," Pauline said. "They sold all the furniture, the silver, the woodwork, the light fixtures, everything. The whole town was crawling with antique dealers. It went on for days. Terrible."

We went outside. It was cloudy and smelled like rain. We got in Pauline's car and drove down the long drive.

The country club was north of town. The road connecting the town to the interstate was lined with fast-food joints and tanning parlors. I told Pauline about missing the exit from the old highway and discovering Jack Braddock in his gas station.

"He's a bum," she said. "He sits out there all day smoking dope and reading books. When he runs out of money, he paints a house or embalms somebody."

"Who did he marry?"

"That's right. You had a thing for him once, didn't you?"

"Not really. I just used to see him all the time. You know how the town boys used to drive around the campus all the time."

"He was a bum even then. He married Kathy Hermann. You probably didn't know her. You'll see her tonight. She's always at the club. Jack too, for that matter. She dumped him for being so lazy."

The wind was blowing and the sky had turned green. Pauline turned on the radio to get a weather report. "We're supposed to have a tornado."

"Good." I love violent weather.

The dining room at the country club was crowded, but Jack Braddock and his former wife were not there. Pauline had gotten me in the mood to watch a battle between ex-spouses, but it was not to be.

"Is the chicken-fried steak good?" Not a typical country club menu item.

"Everything's good. The chef used to be at the Kansas City Country Club."

"Why did he come down here?" To this corn field.

"To be executive chef, I think. Why does anyone come down here? Why am I still here? Cranking out stories on barn restorations when I could be in Kansas City writing God knows what great stuff."

"Barn restorations?"

"That's the fad."

We ate dinner, had a few drinks, watched the storm. We avoided the subject of Sister Barbara. Finally, Pauline said, "My husband's out of town. More or less permanently. We can go to my house to talk."

Pauline's house was in the woods behind the country club. It was modern, the opposite of the Victorian house she had grown up in. A vast window gave us a view of the lightning.

Pauline poured me a glass of vintage port. She sat down on a leather chair and put her legs over the arm. Without looking at me, she said, "My dad forced Barbara to enter the convent. And Tommy to go to the seminary. My dad was a nut case. You met him."

I remembered Pauline's dad. Peter Ross was tall and had one of those long, thin heads that looked like it was stuck in the birth canal too long. A cruel face.

"He made a ton of money when he was still a kid. In the thirties. His grandfather left him a little oil well in Oklahoma, and my dad traded it for a couple more. The guys who traded him thought they were screwing a little kid who didn't know shit, but it turned out the wells came in, and he was a millionaire by the time he was eighteen. He wheeled and dealed and traded some more. That was the early thirties. Everybody else in Oklahoma was broke. Dust bowl. Grapes of Wrath. Busted. My dad got richer and richer. In 1937, he went to New York and found my mother working behind the glove counter at Saks Fifth Avenue. She was a scatterbrained little thing. Just what he wanted. Somebody he could dominate. Mold. I know you've met my mother."

The rain was coming down in torrents, and lightning illuminated the trees bending in the wind. Inside, the lights flickered. Pauline got up and lit a couple of candles in case the power went off.

"My parents got married in 1938. They were both twenty-two. My dad wanted a newspaper. He didn't need to work. He could just indulge himself. Be an editor. Have influence. Impose his nutty views on people. Be the richest guy in town. Have his wife be the queen of local society. There were papers for sale all over the country. Everything was for sale, of course. My dad chose Kansas because of the thing he had for William Allen White. He heard about the *Braddock Herald*. It was an old paper. From the glory days of bleeding Kansas. The *Herald* supported Lincoln. The Union. Abolition. There was lots of activity in Braddock in the old days. That's why the town has two hotels. Everybody was fanatic. A northerner wouldn't stay in the same hotel with a southerner. Hatred. Especially right after the Civil War. Guys from Missouri, bushwhackers, would farm all day, and then cross the state line at night, and come over here, and burn down barns, and poison wells, and tar and feather people. All kinds of stuff. The papers covered it all. My dad bought the *Herald*. The other paper had already gone broke by then.''

''Your dad forced Barbara to enter the convent?''

''He was a crank. He figured that because he got rich at a time when everybody else was going broke, he was smarter than everyone else. What my dad thinks is right, *is* right. Not only politically, but as far as religion goes, too. He used the paper to expound his political notions, anti-Roosevelt, of course. And anti-Truman. God, he hated Truman. But the Catholic thing, he couldn't write about that in the paper. Braddock is Protestant. They don't like Catholics here. Dad had to keep that at home. We had the family rosary every night. With him leading the rosary, giving his insights about the mysteries. It took forever. I learned the meaning of the expression, 'bored to tears.' My dad wore all kinds of medals and scapulars and even a special cord around his waist. Remember those knotted cords? For purity? Remember that weird priest who gave us those cords at retreat senior year? My dad actually wore one of those. He belonged to about fifty different confraternities and third orders. Each one with its little chaplet and booklet and ritual. He was a nut case. He programmed Barb and Tommy from the day they were born. They had no choice. Barbara didn't want to be a nun. She couldn't stand the nuns. She hated St. Adelaide's. She would have been happier at Braddock High. She wanted to go to college. Vassar. She begged my dad. No way. He told her she had to enter the convent. She tried to compromise. She begged him to let her go to college first, and then she would enter the convent. He wouldn't stand for it. I think there was a sexual thing about it. I think he was afraid she'd lose her virginity if she went to college. He was always talking about how great it would be to be a bride of Christ. When she received the habit, he wrote a big thing about it in the paper, the symbolism of the ceremony, all that kind of stuff.''

"Where was your mother in all this?"

"My mother was his puppet. All she cared about was going to Kansas City. To the Plaza. Downtown. Shopping. Harzfeld's. Lunch at the Terrace Grill. The hairdresser. All she cared about was looking good. She did what he told her to do. She said what he wanted her to say. A puppet."

The rain and the thunder and lightning stopped. Pauline opened a window, and cool fresh air rushed into the room. I was very tired, and tired of listening to the bitter story of the Ross family. I knew there was more.

"My sister killed herself. She was miserably unhappy in the convent. She started losing weight from the day she entered. Anorexia. Before she made vows, she told my parents she wanted to come home. Leave the convent. My dad went nuts. Told her she'd be a Judas. He said that since Tommy did everything she did, he'd end up leaving the seminary and be a Judas, too. Dad got the idea that Barb should be a missionary. He paid for Barbara and Sharon to go to Guatemala. He thought the excitement of being the first Adelaide missionary would keep her in the convent. Mother Celeste loved the idea. That was the fad then. Lots of orders that had never been in the missionary business before were sending people down to Latin America to interfere with the local cultures. It was right after the Vatican Council. The orders were booming. Lots of impressionable kids were entering convents. Like the Peace Corps. St. Ad's had the biggest novitiate classes ever when we were in school. Remember how many novices and postulants they had? It was the golden age. It couldn't last, of course. Some nuns and priests were already leaving, but so many were entering, that nobody noticed. Barbara was smart. She could see what was happening. She wanted out of the convent, and she wanted to get away from my dad's influence. She liked Guatemala and her kids down there, but she was too frail, mentally and physically. She came back sick. She had tried to get Dad to let her leave before first vows, and before final vows, but he had too much invested in his image. He was the father of a nun and a priest. He was a Knight of the Holy Sepulcher. He and my mother spent a whole summer once getting the right clothes to wear at a papal audience. Barb killed herself. She had no other way to escape.''

"How did she do it?''

"I think she took pills. She had some really strong pills, little silver ones, from Guatemala. The doctors down there don't worry about people becoming addicts. On the day Barb died, Sharon told us there were no pills found in her room. I figured that meant there were.

Why would she go out of her way to say there were *no* pills?''

"They didn't find a note?''

"No. At least that's what they said. If Barbara left a note, they burned it. Or hid it. Maybe Mother Celeste still has it.''

"Why didn't they do an autopsy?''

"My dad wouldn't hear of it. And Mother Celeste didn't want an autopsy either. I think they both knew Barbara killed herself. It would have been a scandal. This town is really anti-Catholic. It's like the nuns were here on sufferance. The nuns always maintained a low profile. From the beginning. When they first came here, the convent was outside of town. It was only in the twenties that the town built up out to the campus. The townsfolk put up with a convent in their midst because the boarders spent a certain amount of money in town, but there's always been an undercurrent of anti-Catholicism. The Braddocks in particular never liked having the nuns here. They were old New England Puritans. Abolitionists. They never liked papists.''

"I thought Mother Celeste was a relative of the Braddocks.''

"She is. Her mother was a Braddock. Lorena. The black sheep of the family. She disgraced the family when she married a Catholic. Patrick Walsh. An Irishman. And then, Mother Celeste's sister married a Braddock. Married back into the family. Stella Walsh married her first cousin. Henry Braddock. Eddie Braddock was their kid. An idiot from inbreeding. The few surviving Braddocks, Eddie and Jack and Jack's brother Al, are Catholic, but the old ones were all Protestant.''

We heard a sound outside. A bird was calling out with a pure, piercing song. Pauline beckoned to me, and we tiptoed out onto the deck to hear more. "It's a whip-poorwill," she said.

We listened. The sky had cleared, and stars filled the sky. The whippoorwill's call, rich and clear, and the starry sky, and the sad story of a nun's suicide made me cry. Pauline couldn't see my face in the dark. After a while, she said, "You can spend the night, or I can drive you back. Whatever you want."

"Do you mind driving me back?"

"Not at all."

We went back by the old highway. The lights were on in Jack Braddock's filling station. We drove past, and through the back gate to St. Adelaide's.

"What do you think Mother Celeste wants me to do?"

"I'm not sure," Pauline said. "When she had me out here last week, I figured she was going to tell me there was a note or something. But then she told me she was going to get you down here to give her some professional advice. I think she's afraid my parents will sue or something if she tells the truth. Maybe she figures less shit will hit the fan if an investigator from Kansas City breaks the news. It would look like she had you do an investigation, and you just now discovered the truth, that Mother Celeste really didn't know the truth all these years, that you just discovered it. That way she can cover her own ass to the very end. She got you down here to do her dirty work. If it looks like you discovered that Barbara committed suicide, my parents will get mad at *you*, not at Mother Celeste. They'll kill the messenger."

I went inside, and Pauline drove away. There was a dim light burning on the stairway, a Zita touch, to light my way upstairs. In my room, she had turned down my bed and put a plate of cookies and a carton of orange juice on the desk.

I ate the cookies and thought about the whippoorwill. I had never heard one before, although my dad once told me about their sound. No day bird had such a loud call. Was it bad luck or good luck to hear one? It could only be good luck to hear something so beautiful.

I decided to call my answering machine. I went back downstairs and out to my car. I started the engine and dialed the phone. Two unimportant messages. I found myself turning the car around and driving out the back gate. I drove up the road to the gas station. The lights were still on. I pulled up to the pump.

Jack came outside. "It's my lucky day," he said. "I don't see you for twenty-five years, and now I see you three times in one day. Or is it tomorrow?"

"You're working late."

"I usually stay open till midnight. I've got a guy that works for me, keeps it open till ten. Then I come out and close up. But tonight, with the storm, it was so peaceful out here, I just stuck around. What time is it?"

"One."

"You want some gas?"

"Please." I got out of the car.

Jack filled the tank, and checked the oil. I handed him my credit card and followed him into the station. It smelled like marijuana inside. The joint he had been smoking was in an ashtray on the desk. "Want to smoke that jay?" he asked.

"Okay."

He lit it and inhaled deeply. He passed it to me, and I took a couple of hits. "Hold on to that," he said.

"Nice dope."

"Local."

"Excellent."

"How's Mother Celeste?"

"I saw her this afternoon. She doesn't look too bad, but supposedly she's not going to live much longer."

"She's my great-aunt. Did you know that?"

"I think I knew that. I remember you used to serve mass."

"My grandmother and Mother Celeste were sisters."

"Who's the nephew who visits her?"

"Ed Braddock. My uncle. Uncle Eddie. Fast Eddie. President of the Bank of Braddock. How'd you hear about him?"

"One of the nuns mentioned him. I think he was there this morning when I got there."

"Drives a black B.M.W." Jack rolled another jay. We went outside, and stood by my car inhaling the cool air and the sweet marijuana. "Somebody told me you're a detective. Is that true?"

"Private."

"You seem kind of refined for that."

"Most of my stuff is research. Kansas City was an adoption mill in the forties and fifties, and lots of people come back nowadays to find their birth records. I help them. I spend a lot of time in the library."

"You got a gun?"

"I've got two guns. My dad had a couple of guns, and I guess I inherited them with the agency. I've never shot anybody."

"I've got a couple of shotguns and a rifle. My brother's got a handgun at the funeral home. In case someone tries to break in."

We started laughing at that. The idea of someone breaking into a funeral home seemed hilarious.

FIVE

THE ANGELUS woke me in the morning. When I was in school, I could sleep through it, but now I was out of practice. I lay in my narrow bed listening to the bell. Three slow, three slow, three slow, and then thirty-three fast. After the ringing stopped, I heard other morning sounds once familiar. Roosters crowed in the barnyard, and birds sang in the trees outside my window.

I was starving. I went downstairs and took a shower. When I got back to my room, Sister Zita was waiting for me. She had made my bed. "Come over to Father's house when you're dressed," she said, "and I'll fix your breakfast."

I walked across the lilac field to the chaplain's residence. The chaplain was at the motherhouse preparing for mass. I sat down at the little kitchen table and watched Zita fry bacon and eggs. She said, "Mother had a bad night last night. It won't be long now."

"Who told you?"

"I saw Sister Jeanette in the laundry this morning. She was washing Mother's sheets and gowns."

"I'm supposed to see her at eleven."

"How did she seem yesterday?"

"Not bad. I was surprised."

"Sister Jeanette said she cried all night." Zita poured coffee for me and put a couple of slices of convent bread in the toaster.

After breakfast, I went over to the motherhouse to see if I could find Sharon. The mass hadn't ended yet, so I wandered through the halls. The convent looked different from when I was in school. Then there were no ornaments around other than religious pictures, but now there were several knickknack cases filled with collections of bells, mice, and elephants. Porcelain junk. Ceramics. Some of the nuns apparently had allowed the long-suppressed instinct for homemaking to emerge. The cheap figurines looked incongruous in the dark, solemn corridors. A huge picture of Rachel at the well that I had coveted since the first time I saw it still hung by the office door, but another picture I remembered of French Adelaides going to the guillotine was gone.

The chapel doors opened, and the nuns straggled out. In my school days they came out in two lines. They wore black serge habits then, even on days like this. Now, most wore cotton dresses. Some were in slacks. A few wore some remnant of the old habit or the short veil from the transitional habit of the seventies.

Sharon saw me and came down the hall. She took my hand and led me into the alumnae room. "Come down to breakfast with me?"

"No, thanks. Zita fed me already."

"What time are you seeing Mother?"

"Eleven."

"Do you think she wants you to investigate something?"

"I can't figure out what she wants."

"What are you going to do until eleven?"

"Look around. Who collects mice?"

"Isn't that tacky?"

"It's cute. Go to breakfast. I'll be fine. Are you going to take me to Mother's room at eleven?"

"Yes. Meet me in here, okay?"

Sharon left, and I walked around the big room, admiring the antique wicker: chairs, rockers, settees, tables, plant stands. The whole room was filled with white wicker, each piece with cushions covered in white and embroidered with the blue *A* and the gold crown. There was a rack of class pictures at the back of the room. I looked at the young Mother Celeste in the class of '13, a beautiful Gibson Girl in a white shirtwaist.

I found Sharon Bieralski, class of '55. She had her dark hair in a perfect pageboy. Barbara Ross, class of '57, was wearing pearls and a sweater. Her eyes were sad.

I looked at my own picture. I had long, straight hair, a proto-hippie. Pauline Ross looked exactly like Barbara. Her eyes were sad, too.

I went back to the old convent. The library on the second floor was locked, but the key hung on a hook next to the door. I went in. Nothing had changed since the academy closed, although somebody, probably Zita, kept the floor and tables dusted. The magazines on the current issues rack were from 1977. Bing Crosby had just died.

I went through the stacks, looking for old favorites, books that had made boarding school nights and weekends tolerable. I found several old books by the Jesuit, Francis Finn, a great-uncle or something of my dad's. They were boarding school stories from an era when little boys would do anything to avoid being considered mollycoddles. I had read them all, the only person ever to do so. My name was on the checkout cards in the books, several times on each. My handwriting was rounder then, and at various times I used purple, brown, and green ink in my Esterbrook.

The library had been the chapel when the old convent was the only convent, and St. Adelaide stood regnant in a stained-glass window above the checkout desk. Her crown and queenly garb were splendid in the morning sun. I went up the steps into the sanctuary. I sat at the desk and checked out *Tom Playfair.*

I went outside, got in my car, and dialed my answering machine. There were a few messages, and I made a few phone calls.

I drove uptown. There were pickup trucks parked all around the square. Farmers still came to town on Saturdays to shop.

There was a funeral at Braddock Brothers. Several cars were in the parking lot, and a hearse and two black Cadillacs were at the side door.

I parked across the street, in front of the Ross house. I thought about going up to the door and knocking. Did you force your daughter to enter the convent? Did you make her stay when she wanted to leave? Did you drive her to suicide? Did you kill her to protect your image as a Knight of the Holy Sepulcher?

The door opened, and Peter Ross came out. He was wearing a seersucker suit and a straw hat. The perfect picture of a small-town editor of fifty years ago. He walked confidently, not like a man pushing eighty. He came down the walk, opened the gate in the iron fence, and came out onto the sidewalk. He latched the gate behind him and walked past my car. He crossed the street and walked across the square, past the statue of the Union militiaman, past the bandstand, past some kids splashing in a puddle. He went into the *Herald* office.

Someone came up beside me. Jack Braddock. "Are you staking out the Rosses?"

"No, Jack. I'm following *you.* I don't think I've ever seen you in a suit before."

"I'm taking a guy for his last ride in a half an hour. I've got to look sharp."

"You drive the hearse?"

"Slow and steady. You got home okay last night?"

"Slow and steady."

"I'd like to take you to dinner tonight. Would that be a possibility? Are you going to be around?"

"That would be very nice. Thank you."

"Great. Would you like to go to the country club again?"

"Again?" I hadn't told him about dinner with Pauline Ross.

"I'm following you too, Frances. Or at least my spies are." He pointed to a man standing by one of the funeral cars. "Rudy. He drives for us and tends bar at the country club."

"Could I let you know for sure this afternoon? I'm not sure what I'm going to be doing. They might have plans for me at St. Ad's that they haven't told me about yet."

"Sure. I'll be at the station this afternoon. What about lunch at Harley's to finalize plans for dinner?"

"I'll try to make it. If not, I'll speak to you this afternoon."

Rudy was motioning to Jack. "Got to go," Jack said. "See you later."

I got out of my car, and walked around the square. Through the window of the *Herald* office, I could see Peter Ross sitting at a desk, reading the paper. I didn't see Pauline. The *Herald* was a weekly now; it came out on Saturdays. I bought a copy from the box outside the office, and went to Harley's to read it. The drugstore was full of farmers and their kids. There was no place to sit, so I got a cup of coffee to go and went to the

square. I read Pauline's story about the planned reno-
vation of the Southern Hotel. I read the obituary of the
man just now being driven by Jack to the cemetery west
of town. I read the unfamiliar comic strips and the auc-
tion notices. Finally, Peter Ross came out of the *Herald*
office, and crossed the street. He retraced his path across
the square. He passed my bench and looked at me with
his cruel eyes. There was no sign of recognition.

I waited until he was back inside his house. Then I
walked back to my car and drove back to St. Ad's. I
went upstairs to my room. Zita had put fresh flowers in
the vase.

I climbed out on the fire escape to think. I could see
the kitchen sisters in the garden and an old nun in the
apple orchard doing something to the beehives. Two
nuns were sitting in wheelchairs on the motherhouse
porch.

What was Mother Celeste going to ask me to do?
What should I charge? My dad told me once never to
work for the clergy. A priest he had done some investigating for once had stiffed him, refused to pay his bill.
Would that apply to nuns, too? Still, I was good at looking into the past. Searching through old birth records,
old newspapers, old city directories, old letters, that was
what I did best. The idea of questioning the nuns and
the Ross family about a death that had occurred thirty
years ago appealed to me.

I thought about Sister Barbara. I had spoken to her
only once. I used to get sick at mass nearly every morning when I was in boarding school. My body would
scream for release from the long, boring service. I
would start feeling faint. I would sit down, but that
wouldn't be enough. I would have to go outside. Sometimes, if I waited too long to go outside, I would faint

when I reached the convent porch. If I got out in time, I would sit down on the steps, and put my head down to get the oxygen flowing to my brain again. Once when I was doing that, Sister Barbara came out a door at the far end of the porch, from what I now knew was the nuns' infirmary. She was dressed the way our dorm nuns dressed at night, in a black flannel robe over white pajamas with a short, night veil on her head. She bent down, and put her hand on my forehead. Even though there was snow on the ground, I was hot and clammy. "Are you okay?" she asked. Her voice was deep like Pauline's, only softer. "Do you want me to get Sister Jeanette?"

"No, thank you," I said. "I'm fine. I just got a little dizzy. I'm going over to the dorm in a minute." To sit with Zita in the infirmary, and listen to gossip, and drink tea.

"You shouldn't be sitting on this wet stone," Sister Barbara said. She helped me stand up. Her hands were very thin. She brushed the snow off my uniform.

I went down the steps after that and over to the old convent. Zita was not in the infirmary. I went upstairs to my room. I looked out the window. Sister Barbara was still standing on the motherhouse porch.

Had she killed herself to escape convent life? In 1965, there were fewer options for women than there are today, and she may have been so weakened by starvation and pressure from her parents that she couldn't think straight. If it had gotten out that she had killed herself, they might have denied her a Christian burial. They might have buried her at the crossroads with a stake in her heart or something. Why would anyone murder her?

A black B.M.W. came up the long drive. Eddie Braddock parked in front of the motherhouse and went up
the steps.

SIX

"FRANCES, I'D LIKE you to meet my nephew, Mr. Edgar Braddock. Eddie, this is Ms. Frances Finn."

I could see no resemblance either to Mother Celeste or to Jack. Eddie Braddock had neither curly hair nor perfect teeth. He was in his late fifties, short, overweight. He was wearing brown leather loafers on his tiny feet. He had on khaki slacks and a purple shirt with a polo player on the front. He was wearing a signet ring.

"This is most unfortunate," he said. "If only Sister Sharon had told me you were driving down here, I could have nipped this in the bud."

Mother Celeste said, "Eddie doesn't approve of my hiring a private investigator."

"There's nothing to investigate. There's no reason to open this can of worms at this point in time."

"I have to take care of this before I die," Mother Celeste said.

"Nonsense. You're going to outlive us all. Ms. Finn, if you will submit a bill for the time you've been here, I'll reimburse you, but there's no question of going on..."

Mother Celeste cut him off in the strong voice I remembered from the past. "That's enough, Eddie. Frances has come to help me."

"Ms. Finn," Eddie said, "I understand you were a student here once upon a time. You are aware, no doubt, of my aunt's flair for the dramatic?"

"Frances," Mother Celeste said, "what is your fee schedule? Do we begin by paying you a retainer?"

"I charge by the case, Mother. You haven't told me what you want me to do yet."

"I'm very weak," Mother Celeste said. "I had planned to take care of this matter myself, but since the operation, I'm so weak. I can't think straight. Sometimes I try to think about something, and the pain takes away the thought before I finish it. I've waited too long. I have to ask you to do something I should have done myself years ago."

Eddie said, "My aunt has gotten the notion into her head that Barbara Ross was murdered. There's no question of that, of course. And if it were true, which it isn't, what would be the point of dredging it up now? There would be no possibility of bringing the killer to justice. And even if there were, the bishop has a man, a discreet investigator, on retainer. The last thing we need..."

"Were you acquainted with Sister Barbara, Mr. Braddock?" I asked.

"Certainly. I was a few years older than the twins, but we lived across the street. We went to the same school. St. George's. I often walked home from school with Barbara and Tommy. I bought lemonade from their lemonade stands. Sometimes..."

He was twinkling with memories, but Mother Celeste cut him off. "I have no intention of bringing the killer to justice. God is just. God will take care of that in eternity. But I want the killer to know that I know."

"Who was it?" I thought I might try again to get an answer.

"I'm not going to tell you, Frances," the old nun said. She tried to smile, to show me the white teeth that had survived a century, but the pain twisted her mouth into a grimace.

"My aunt is afraid you might let the cat out of the bag."

"Cat?"

"You might glance at the guilty party at the meeting," Eddie said. "Or even avoid glancing at the guilty party. That would give it away, too. She won't even tell *me* who it is she suspects."

"Meeting?"

"I want you to conduct a meeting, Frances," Mother Celeste said. "I want you to speak to those concerned. Sister Barbara's family. The nuns. I want you to assure everyone that Sister Barbara did not take her own life. Tell them she was murdered."

"You want me to announce that Sister Barbara was murdered?"

"That's right."

"Without saying who murdered her?"

"Yes."

"Absurd," Eddie Braddock said.

"You want me to say that you know who murdered her, but that you do not intend to name the killer?"

"Exactly."

"It's ridiculous, isn't it?" Eddie Braddock said.

I wasn't ready to agree with him. "Mother, what makes you think Sister Barbara was murdered?"

"I saw the murderer coming out of the infirmary that morning. At five o'clock. The murderer didn't know I was in the hall. We didn't find Sister Barbara's body until nine. I never told anyone that I had seen someone coming out of the infirmary four hours earlier."

"I'm not sure why that proves Sister Barbara was murdered."

"It proves nothing, obviously." Eddie said. "My aunt has never been able to face the fact that a sister would commit suicide. Therefore, she's come up with this theory…"

"I'm not trying to prove it, Frances," Mother Celeste said. "I know it. If I told you the murderer's name and certain other circumstances, you would believe me. But it's not important that you believe me. The important thing is clearing Sister Barbara's name. The more important thing is getting the murderer to go to confession. You should reassure everyone that the murderer poses no threat to anyone else. I'm sure of that. The circumstances were very particular."

"I'm a Braddock, Ms. Finn," Eddie said. "You're from Kansas City, so you can't appreciate what that means in this town. Actually, I'm a double Braddock." He held out his hand, and looked at his signet ring. "This is not seemly. This could get out. As it is, my aunt is respected in this town. She's a Braddock on her mother's side. I can't permit her to jeopardize her position. It's my duty to prevent this fantasy from going beyond this room. I only hope you have the integrity to keep this under your hat. Barbara Ross was the hysterical, spoiled daughter of an extremely unpleasant and eccentric man. It's unfortunate that she died at an early age, but these things happen. The Rosses are getting up in years, and the last thing they want is for people to be talking about their daughter's death again."

Mother Celeste said, "At the meeting, Frances, just say, 'Mother Celeste saw someone coming out of Sister Barbara's room that morning. The morning of her death. Mother Celeste has never told anyone. Because she is a coward. That is her besetting fault. But she knows what happened. She has known all these years. And

God knows. And Sister Barbara in heaven knows. The murderer must go to confession. Before it's too late.'"

"The murderer will be at the meeting?" That meant the murderer was one of the nuns or one of the Rosses. Was I beginning to believe Mother Celeste? "The others might wonder why you expect them to continue on with a murderer in their midst. And I'm not sure that I want to be in a room with a murderer. Especially if I don't know who it is."

"It's too absurd," Eddie said. "Someone might take it seriously and run out and call the police. That's all we need. Imagine Randy Hermann out here, questioning us all about murder. Imagine how Peter Ross would react to that."

"Ask them to come tonight, Frances," Mother Celeste said. "Peter and Winnie Ross. Tommy. Pauline. The nuns."

"Most of the nuns who were here when Barbara Ross was alive left the convent years ago," Eddie said. "You're left with a skeleton crew. The nuns are not interested in this. They've forgotten all about it. And why is it necessary to draw an outsider into it?" Eddie gave me a dirty look and marched over to the door in his little brown loafers. "We don't need an outsider to conduct this séance. I will be happy to tell the nuns and the Rosses that you're convinced Barbara died a natural death, as most people believe anyway. Anyone who suspected her of suicide is simply wrong. And no one blames her, anyway. A person who commits suicide when she's sick and on medication is not responsible. Even the Church admits that. She was sick. She wasn't herself. You said that yourself. No one would hold her responsible. She could have misjudged the amount of her medicine. She may…"

I interrupted him. "Mother, if you want me to talk to Sister Barbara's family and the nuns, I'll do it. But I don't think it's a good idea to mention murder. I'm an investigator by trade. I make my living at it. I prefer to do things my own way. It would be unprofessional of me to make insinuations about something I'm not sure about. Something I haven't investigated myself and drawn conclusions about. It could hurt me professionally. I *am* willing to conduct a meeting, however. And I would be willing to investigate the circumstances of Sister Barbara's death, if you want me to do that."

Eddie snorted. "Unbelievable."

"I don't want you to investigate," Mother Celeste said. "It's not necessary. There's nothing to investigate."

"Then why don't I just say at the meeting that you want to assure everyone that Sister Barbara did not commit suicide? I'll say you're determined to make that clear. I'll say you're not prepared to give reasons for your conclusion, but that you want anyone who thinks Sister Barbara killed herself to be aware that she did not. If someone at the meeting is a murderer, the fact that you have gone to all this trouble will alert that person that you know the truth. The others will just assume that in your position as mother superior, you're told lots of things in confidence that you can't divulge fully to other people."

"This is absurd," Eddie said. "I won't stand by and watch this." He looked at his watch.

"If you want the meeting tonight, I'd better get on the phone," I said.

Mother Celeste started crying. Big tears rolled down her cheeks. "Please come back at three and tell me what you've arranged. I need to be alone now."

Eddie Braddock followed me out the door to the porch. "Really, Ms. Finn, this is unbelievable. You can't go phoning people and spreading this thing around. I have standing in this town. My aunt isn't herself. Let's give her a few days to recover from the surgery. When she feels better, she'll forget all about this. It's the after-effects of the anesthesia talking. She's on painkillers. You go on home. Send me your bill for the twenty-four hours you've been here."

I was shaking with nerves. I was tempted to do what he said. I was out of my depth. This little man, tapping his way down the stone steps beside me, was about to succeed in persuading me to leave the dead to bury the dead. It would be pleasant to get back to my house and back to my work. There, my biggest challenges involved persuading an occasional courthouse clerk to give me a peek at an old birth certificate, or paying a file clerk to let me copy a page from a medical record or a college transcript.

We reached my car. I opened the trunk, and got out my briefcase. "You're going to be responsible for paying my bill?" I asked. I took out a contract and began filling it in. I handed it to him.

He took a long time to read it. "Is this your usual fee for this kind of thing?"

"This kind of thing isn't usual. But I'm willing to do a favor for Mother Celeste for old times' sake. Since I'm not investigating anything, just addressing a meeting, I'm giving you a break on the fee. You handle the convent's financial matters?"

"The convent is in dire straits," Eddie said. "I try to protect them from people who would take advantage of them."

"Mother Celeste seems to feel that this is important.

I can understand why. I didn't realize that Sister Barbara was suspected of having committed suicide.''

"Of course she committed suicide. Why bring it up now? My aunt reads too many Agatha Christies. The idea of murder is obnoxious. I'm amazed that you would take advantage…"

"That's the second time you've used that term, Mr. Braddock. I'm not taking advantage of anyone. I respect Mother Celeste enough to give credence to what she thinks.''

"She's not in her right mind. Anyone can see that. I'm not saying she's senile. She's full of painkillers. She's dying, and she's scared. To stir up ancient history because of an old woman's deathbed fixation could be dangerous. Peter Ross is a litigious man. You might be biting off more than you can chew.''

I closed the trunk and put the briefcase on top. I handed Eddie Braddock a pen. "You suspect Peter Ross?''

"Of what? I don't suspect anyone of anything. Nothing happened.''

"What do you mean, 'litigious'?''

"I'm a banker, Ms. Finn. In a town like Braddock, that's like being a priest or a psychiatrist. I'm privy to lots of secrets that I have no intention of sharing with an outsider.''

"Has he ever sued *you?*''

"I'm late for dinner. I'll meet you in my aunt's room at three o'clock. We'll decide then whether or not to proceed with this charade. Or whether to let sleeping dogs lie.'' He took another look at the contract. "Are you deducting the cost of the food and shelter we're providing while you're here?''

I didn't answer. Who's *we?*

He scrawled his name on the contract.

"Speaking of priests," I said, "where is Tommy Ross?"

"He's been pastor of St. George's for ten years."

SEVEN

I DROVE UPTOWN and parked in front of the Ross house again. The hearse and the black Cadillacs were back in the lot at Braddock Brothers.

I walked around the square and went into Harley's.

Jack Braddock was in a booth. He waved to me to join him. He was still in his black funeral suit. "Are we on for tonight?"

"Yes, I'm looking forward to it. I have to go to a meeting with some of the nuns at seven, but I'll be free at eight. Is that too late?"

"No, that's great. I've got to get out to the station, now. The kid that works for me has to leave. I'll pick you up at St. Ad's at eight, okay?"

"I'm staying in the old convent."

"I'll ring the bell."

"Don't you dare."

Jack left, and I moved to an empty seat at the counter. I didn't want to hog a booth while families were waiting to sit down. I made some notes on a paper napkin while I waited for my cheeseburger.

Whodunit? It had to be one of the nuns. Mother Celeste would not have watched anyone else coming out of a room in the infirmary, even a member of Sister Barbara's family, at five o'clock in the morning, and not challenged him. Or her. The cloister was carefully observed in those days, and no one but the nuns ever went down that corridor. Even if a member of a sick nun's family or a doctor or a priest was allowed down there, that person wouldn't have been there at five o'clock in the morning. And Mother Celeste wouldn't feel that God would hold her responsible for the sin of someone not under her direction.

What was *she* doing in the hall at five o'clock in the morning? The nuns got up at five-thirty in those days. Why was Mother Celeste sneaking around, lurking around in the dark? Why didn't she show herself, and say to the nun coming out of the infirmary, "Are you checking on Sister Barbara? How is she feeling this morning?" Why didn't Mother Celeste go into Sister Barbara's room herself to check on her?

Why would one of the nuns kill Sister Barbara? Why would Mother Celeste allow a killer nun to stay in the convent, endangering everyone?

What exactly had happened on the morning of Sister Barbara's death? I remembered Sister Vivian, our dorm prefect, telling us that day that Sister Barbara had been found dead in her bed by one of the nuns who went in to check on her. It was quite late in the morning—late for nuns, that is. Nine o'clock. Barbara had been sick, and nearly always slept late. No one had missed her at morning prayers, mass, or breakfast. She rarely got up for any of those.

If one of the nuns killed Sister Barbara, why drag the Rosses into it? I hated to agree with Eddie Braddock, but why not let sleeping dogs lie? I didn't like calling Barbara Ross, who once had been kind to me, a dog.

Pauline came into Harley's and stood behind me. She ordered a cup of coffee to go.

"Hello, Pauline."

"What's going on at St. Adelaide's?" A farmer moved down a stool, and Pauline sat beside me.

"Mother Celeste wants me to invite you and your

brother and your parents to a meeting tonight. Seven o'clock in the alumnae room.''

The farmer pricked up his weatherbeaten ears, so I spoke softly. ''A little discussion. Can you make it?''

''Sure. You've talked to Tom and my parents?''

''Not yet.''

''You want me to call them?''

My cheeseburger and hashed browns came. I worked at applying ketchup and mustard. ''I thought I might just drop in on them. Would that be okay? My car is parked right in front of your parents' house. There weren't any spaces on the square.''

''Sure, that's fine. Let me know if you need me to twist any arms.'' Pauline paid for her coffee and left.

After I finished my lunch, I walked back to my car and phoned for my messages. While I made a few calls, I looked at the Rosses' house. Every shade was drawn precisely to the middle of every window. Every lace curtain was tied back with a big, blue bow. The yard was planted lavishly with peonies and irises.

I walked up to the house, and rang the doorbell.

Winnie Ross opened the door. She was tiny and blonde, dressed in a tan linen dress and high heels. She looked at me as if she recognized me.

''Good afternoon, Mrs. Ross. My name is Frances Finn. I was in Pauline's class at St. Adelaide's. I don't know if you remember me or not.''

''Of course I remember you, Frances. How lovely to see you again. Please come in.''

The hardwood floors gleamed with wax, and the walls were painted yellow. The chintz slipcovers on the chairs and sofas were yellow and blue.

''Sit down, dear. Does Pauline know you're in town? She's at the paper. She'll be delighted. Why don't I call her? Let me get you some lemonade first. It's so hot. All the rain just makes it hotter."

Peter Ross came into the living room from the library. Winnie introduced us. He stared at me with cold eyes. "Pauline mentioned that you were in Braddock," he said. "You're visiting Mother Celeste?"

"Yes, that's right. Mother Celeste sent me to invite you and Mrs. Ross to a meeting this evening."

Winnie said, "A meeting? About what, dear?"

"About Sister Barbara's death."

"About the memorial fund?"

"Memorial fund?" What memorial fund?

"My wife and I set up a scholarship fund in our daughter's memory," Peter Ross said. "It paid the tuition every year for two girls to attend St. Adelaide's. Since the academy closed, we've never heard a word about the money. We've been wondering when we'd get an accounting of it."

Winnie Ross said, "I suppose now that Mother Celeste is about to meet her maker, she wants to take care of all her unfinished business."

"I suppose so," I said. "She hasn't given me the exact agenda for the meeting."

They agreed to come. They didn't seem surprised about it or curious about why I had been brought from Kansas City to conduct the meeting. To old people, the thought of taking care of unfinished business seemed reasonable. Winnie repeated her offer of lemonade, but I said I couldn't stay.

Braddock is a small town, but St. George's Church was in an area I was unfamiliar with. My friends and I always kept to the same route on our walks to and from town. This residential neighborhood west of the square was one we never visited. The houses were newer than

those to the east. They had a square, postwar look to
them. I slowed in front of the first church I saw, but it
was Congregationalist. The Catholic church was farther
out, smaller, less prosperous looking.

The man mowing the wet grass was Tommy Ross,
Barbara Ross's twin. He wore a straw hat like his father's. He took it off when I approached him. Old-
fashioned manners. He was wearing a white tee-shirt
and black, clerical pants. He was over six feet tall, like
his father. He had grown very stout since the last time
I saw him. At Barbara's funeral.

"Father Ross?"

"Ms. Finn?" Pauline or his parents must have called
him.

"Yes. Mother Celeste has asked me to invite you to
attend a meeting this evening at the convent."

"About Barbara."

"Yes."

"What more is there to say?"

"I'm not sure. Apparently Mother Celeste feels
something remains to be said. May I tell her you'll be
there?"

"I'll be there."

"Is seven convenient?" He might have confessions
or something on Saturday night.

"Seven is fine. Mother Celeste has employed you to
do her dirty work?"

"Pauline said the same thing. I'm not sure why you
feel that way. Sometimes a disinterested outsider can
handle a situation too emotional for those directly involved."

"What situation are you referring to? The fact that
my sister was murdered?" He saw that he had shocked
me. "I know my sister was murdered. Is Mother Celeste

finally prepared to admit that she's been harboring a murderer all these years?''

"You think one of the nuns murdered Barbara?"

"I don't think it. I know it. Sharon Bieralski killed my sister."

Sharon? Gentle Sharon? My favorite nun? The person who had had a heart attack from the stress of trying to support the dying community? "Why would you say that?"

"I'll explain at the meeting tonight. I'll tell you one thing now though, Ms. Finn. Biologically speaking, Barbara and I were fraternal twins, but spiritually speaking, we were identical. In our hearts, we were one. If my sister had killed herself, I would have known it. I would have felt it. And Barbara would not have left me without saying good-bye. Without even a note." He burst out crying. He cried openly, like a child, without putting his hands to his big face.

"Barbara didn't go to bed at night without writing me a note. When we were little kids, I'd find notes from her under my pillow when I went to bed. I'd find notes in my lunch box at school and in my missal at mass. After Barbara entered the convent, and I was in the seminary, she wrote to me every night. She was only allowed to send me one letter a week, but she wrote every night. I'd get a week's worth of letters at once." He wiped his eyes and his sweating face with a handkerchief. A death that had occurred a long time ago was causing a lot of grief still. "I'm sorry," he said.

"It's all right," I said. I was worried now that this unstable man would get up at the meeting and accuse Sharon of murder. What if he gave her another heart attack? "I guess I don't understand about twins. I don't think anyone can who isn't a twin."

"We started out as one person. When Barbara died, half of me died. I'm frozen in time. I've just been going through the motions ever since. I'm not really alive."

"I don't know if it's a good idea to accuse someone of murder, though. Have you mentioned your suspicions to anyone else?"

"I don't talk about it. I've never talked about it. Even with my parents. They never mention Barbara. It's as if Barbara, half of me, never existed. I'm sorry. Mother Celeste is right. Maybe it *is* time to tell the truth."

"Do you know that Sister Sharon isn't well? She had a heart attack in May."

"She was jealous of Barbara."

"Jealous?"

"Barbara brought her home on her home visit. The summer before she made final vows."

The nuns were allowed a home visit once every five years in the old days. They had to take a companion along, and they could stay with their parents for a week.

"Sharon looked around our house like she had never seen anything like it. Sharon Bieralski from Chicago. A stockyard worker's daughter. How many Polacks does it take to kill somebody? She looked at everything in our house. You could see the envy in her eyes."

The ugly language and the anger in this man's voice over something he imagined had happened more than thirty years ago frightened me.

"Forgive me," he said in a completely different voice. "I've kept you standing here in the sun. Would you like to come in and have a glass of lemonade?"

The last thing on earth I wanted was to go inside his little ranch-type rectory. I had to get back to St. Ad's and warn Sharon. "No, thank you. I'll let you get back to your mowing. I'll see you tonight in the alumnae room?''

"I wouldn't miss it." He wiped his face again.

EIGHT

I DROVE BACK to St. Adelaide's. I went in the mother-house and asked the old nun in the office where Sister Sharon was. She said Sharon was resting. She would be getting up soon. She asked me to wait in the alumnae room.

I stood in front of Barbara Ross's picture again. What had happened in 1965? Pauline was convinced that her older sister had killed herself. Her story of her family had convinced me that she was right. But when Mother Celeste had told me Barbara was murdered, the conviction in her voice had swayed me to believe *her*. I had agreed to go along with her plan for a meeting. In spite of what Eddie Braddock said, I didn't think a dying woman would stage a charade. What would be the point? And Tom Ross? He seemed convinced that Sharon Bieralski was capable of murder, an idea so preposterous that I shivered with fear. How could he think Sharon could kill anyone? And with what motive? Envy over Barbara's parents' house? What had I gotten into? What if Sister Barbara *had* been murdered? That meant I was in danger. The murderer might get worried about being exposed after all these years and kill *me*.

I couldn't stand up in front of the Rosses and say Barbara had been murdered, and Mother Celeste knew who did it, but she didn't want to say who it was. They might call the police. I could get in a mess that would harm me professionally. I was drawn into an emotional mess already. These people were volatile, not altogether sane. I sat down on one of the wicker chairs.

After a while, Sharon came into the room. She looked at me with a question in her eyes.

"Let's go outside," I said. I took her hand and led her outside. We walked around to the gardens.

Sharon had been my favorite nun when I was in school. Every girl in my class had a favorite nun. It was the fad. For some girls, the favorite nun was the object of a crush, but Sharon was not the type for that. I didn't write notes to her and leave them at her place in chapel. She wouldn't have liked that. I didn't pry into her pre-convent life. She was quite open about that and answered any questions I had. Sharon was simple and straightforward about everything.

She was new at the academy my sophomore year. She had just come back from Guatemala, and her experience there had given her a more realistic attitude toward life than many of the nuns had. She was my journalism teacher. I was editor of the *Crown* my junior and senior years, and Sharon and I were together in the journalism room nearly every evening. She would be setting type on the tiny printing press for the *Crown* or the *Alumnae Bulletin* or something. She would have her small sleeves off and her big sleeves pinned up, her graceful arms revealed and her fingers stained with ink. I would be typing a story or laying out a page. I would ask her about her life. She would tell me about her days as a boarder at St. Ad's in the fifties and about her childhood in Chicago. She told me about her father who came from Poland to New York. He got a job on the docks in Brooklyn. He paid two guys to teach him English. They taught him Italian, and he didn't know the difference. Finally, he decided to move to Chicago where he had heard there were lots of Poles. He only knew how to say "bacon and eggs" in English. That's what he ate on the train for three days. Sharon told me about her mother who worked as a cleaning woman in office buildings in Chicago. She saved enough money to send her daughters to boarding school in Kansas. Sharon showed me pictures of her married sisters and her nieces and nephews. I knew Sharon was not jealous of the Rosses. If anything, she probably pitied them.

Sharon had come to my graduation from college, the only nun from St. Ad's to do so. She came to my dad's funeral. She had been my friend from the day we met. The fact that Tom Ross thought she was capable of murder did not make *me* think that. Instead, it made me wonder if *he* had killed his twin sister and was now prepared to make trouble for Sharon.

A weird family's past anger was being stirred up. And Mother Celeste, who never had liked me, suddenly had called me back to St. Adelaide's. She didn't want me to investigate anything, she wanted me to get up in front of a group of people and make insinuations. She wanted the Rosses stirred up more, and the nuns frightened. Why? Why was she spending her last days on earth doing this? I felt no loyalty to Mother Celeste. She was not my client. What she was asking me to do was not my line of work, therefore I had no client. But I had a friend, and I intended to warn her about Tom Ross and Mother Celeste.

We reached the barnyard fence. The cows and horses that had lived there when I was in school were gone. The pigpen was empty. Only chickens remained. They strutted around importantly, pecking the ground. How should I say it? Tom Ross thinks you killed his sister? What if she had another heart attack?

Sharon leaned against the fence. "Remember Beelzebub?" she asked. That was one of the horses the nuns kept for the boarders to ride.

"He tried to kill me once," I said. "He ran under a low branch on a tree."

"You would have been hanging there by your hair like what's his name."

"Absalom."

"What's going on, Frances?"

"Mother Celeste wants a meeting tonight to talk about Sister Barbara's death."

Sharon couldn't have faked the surprise on her face. "Sister Barbara?"

"She wants me to conduct a meeting with the Rosses and the nuns. That's what she wanted me down here for."

"I don't get it."

"Mother Celeste claims Sister Barbara was murdered. She wanted me to get up and tell everyone that. She said if I would do that, the people who think Barbara killed herself would know she didn't, and the killer would go to confession."

"She told you Barbara was *murdered?*"

"She said Barbara was wearing her scapular when they found her. She would never put on her scapular and then kill herself."

Sharon put her hands on my face. She looked into my eyes. "Frances," she said, "I'm sorry I got you into this. I had no idea what she was up to. I thought she wanted you down here to look into a financial situation that has come up. This is unbelievable. A meeting." She turned away from me. She leaned against the fence again.

"Seven o'clock tonight. I've already talked to Pauline and the Rosses and Tom."

"You talked to Tom Ross?"

"A very strange guy."

"They're all strange."

"They're coming. I'm supposed to go back to Mother Celeste at three and confirm the arrangements."

"I can't believe this. She had me get you down here for this? She wants you to get up in front of the nuns and tell them Barbara was murdered? Honey, Sister Barbara wasn't murdered."

"How do you know?"

"Because I found her body. I went in her room at five that morning, and she was dead."

"That was you?"

"What do you mean?"

"Mother Celeste said she saw someone coming out of Barbara's room that morning. The person didn't know she was there. It was you."

"She saw me?"

"I guess so. She must have been lurking around somewhere."

Sharon put her hand on her chest. She closed her eyes and took a deep breath.

"Are you okay?"

"I'm okay. This is just unbelievable. Why is she doing this? She thinks I killed Sister Barbara? How could she think that? For all these years she's been thinking that? She thinks I could *kill* someone?"

"That's what I can't figure out. If she really thought that, why wouldn't she do something? Why would she want to live with a killer? And if she doesn't really think that, why is she doing this? Why get me down here? Why put you through this? Is her mind messed up from drugs? Or from the trauma of the surgery? Or from old age? What is going on? Why would she see you coming out of Barbara's room and assume you killed her? How would she make that leap?"

Sharon took my hand and led me to a bench by the garden shed. We sat down. She said, "I woke up early that morning. Somehow I knew Barbara was in trouble. We had been in Guatemala together, and I knew her. The day before, she had been up all day. Keyed up. She had been in bed for weeks, but that day she was up all day. She ate in the refectory and went to recreation and prayers and everything. Which she never did. I knew her. I knew that after a day of being up, she would be down. Her parents had been out to see her in the afternoon, and she had a long visit with them, and she was all keyed up.

"I woke up at five, and I went over to check on her. I don't know if I had a premonition or what. Something made me get up and go over there. Barbara was dead. It was obvious. Her jaw had fallen. Other things. I put my hand under the blanket, and there was still a little warmth. I said the Act of Contrition in her ear. But she was dead. It was obvious. She had taken pills. She was so sick. I know she didn't know what she was doing. She was so sick. A couple of times in Guatemala she took more pills than she was supposed to. She wasn't responsible. The water glass and the jar were on the table by her bed."

"The jar?"

"The pills came from a doctor in Guatemala. She went to a doctor down there, and he gave her pills. Morphine. In a fruit jar. She took them all the time. She didn't eat. She just took pills. She couldn't teach. She was in bed all the time. We came back. I couldn't do it all myself down there and take care of her on top of it. I tried to get her to stop taking the pills, and she said she would, but she didn't. She got more from the same doctor before we came back. She was addicted.

"Her room was perfectly clean that morning. Barbara was messy ordinarily, but she had cleaned her room perfectly. Everything was in perfect order. She had written notes to everyone: her parents, her brother, Pauline, me. Her rosary and her scapular were on the table. I put the scapular on her and her rosary in her hand. I took the jar the pills had been in and the water glass and the letters. I didn't want people to know she had committed suicide. You don't realize what that would have meant then. Barbara was sick. She didn't realize what she was doing. I left her room and didn't say anything. I knew Jeanette would find her after breakfast. I couldn't do anything. I was too scared. I had to have some time to think. Mother Celeste saw me?"

"Apparently so. I think you should go with me to see her. I'm supposed to see her at three. We'll tell her what really happened. Cancel the meeting."

"She let me be around the kids all these years, and she thought I was a murderer? She has me in there every day running her errands and brushing her teeth, and she thinks I'm a murderer? She doesn't think that, Frances. There's something else going on here, and I know what it is. Something to do with the community. Mother Celeste had no right to drag you into this."

"What do you want me to do?"

Sharon looked at me for a long time. Then she said, "We'll have the meeting. Only *I'll* conduct the meeting. I'll tell them the truth about Barbara's death. Maybe it *is* time for everyone to know the truth. You go on inside and tell Mother Celeste the meeting is all set. Don't worry. I'll take care of it. You don't even have to hang around if you'd rather get out of here. You might want to get home.''

"I've got a date.''

"A date?''

"Jack Braddock is taking me out to dinner.''

"You don't waste time.''

"Where are the notes?'' I knew she would have kept them.

"I have them. I'll bring them to the meeting. Don't say anything to Mother Celeste.''

"How do I let the nuns know about the meeting?''

"I'll pass the word this afternoon. I'll make sure everyone hears about it. Why don't you mention it to Zita? She'll want to set up a refreshment table.''

"There's something else.''

"What?'' She took another deep breath.

"Tom Ross thinks you killed Barbara, too.''

Sharon leaned back against the shed. She said, "Did you ever think the day would come when we'd be sitting out here having a conversation like this?''

"On St. Joseph's bench.'' When I was in school, homeless men, still called hoboes or tramps or bums in those days, would come to the convent for food. They would sit on this bench and wait for Zita or one of the kitchen sisters to notice them. "St. Joseph is here,'' the nuns would say when they saw one of the traveling men. They would take out coffee and a meal on a plastic tray.

"What did he say?''

"He said you were jealous of Barbara. Of the Rosses' riches. When you went with Barbara on her home visit, he noticed you looking at all their stuff.''

"He's a lunatic.''

"I think you might need some advice. I know a very good lawyer in Kansas City. He's helped me with a few things. He could be down here by tonight. Then if Tom Ross starts making accusations, you would have somebody beside you to get up and tell him he's asking for a lawsuit."

"I can handle Tom Ross. I'll give him his sister's letter. That will shut him up."

"Have you read it?"

"No, but I read my own. I'm sure Tommy's is similar."

"I'd like to come to the meeting."

"To hold my hand?"

"To see how everyone reacts. Pauline told me she always thought Barbara committed suicide. And she always thought there were notes, too."

We walked around to the front of the motherhouse. Eddie Braddock's car was parked by the statue of St. Adelaide. It was quarter to three. "I'll go find Zita," I said, "and then I'll come back over here."

"I'll tell the nuns about the meeting. Just be calm. Everything will be all right."

NINE

Zita was in her room. In the founders' days, it had been a parlor. The mantelpiece had been removed from the corner fireplace, and a plain, modern fixture had been put up where an old, brass lamp once had hung.

There was a huge clap of thunder then, and Zita and I both jumped. We started laughing. "Who bought all the fireplaces and stuff?" I asked.

"Antique dealers from all over the place," Zita said. She turned on the light. The rain was starting.

"Maybe we're going to get the tornado today."

"Are you hungry? I have some peanut butter." Zita had gotten the idea years ago that I liked peanut butter, which I don't. Whenever I ditched mass to sit in this little room with her, she would give me peanut butter on convent bread and camomile tea.

"No, thanks. I've got to get over to Mother at three."

"What's going on?"

"There's going to be a meeting tonight at seven."

"A meeting?"

"That's what Mother Celeste wanted me down here for. To arrange a meeting. The nuns and the Ross family. Sharon told me to tell you."

"A meeting with the Rosses?"

"To discuss Sister Barbara's death."

The rain was coming in the window. Zita closed it and wiped the windowsill with a rag. "The Rosses know about it?"

"Yes."

"In the alumnae room?"

"Yes."

"Why did Mother need *you* for that?"

"That's what I'm trying to figure out."

A streak of lightning was followed by another immense thunderclap. Then, loud rumbling went on and on. Zita and I moved away from the window. The storm was right above us. The light flickered, and went out.

"Is my window closed upstairs?"

"I closed it when it started looking like rain."

The trees were bending in the wind. "I've got to go," I said. "Why don't you come down to the tunnel with me? Just in case."

The tunnel was an underground passageway connecting the old convent to the motherhouse. It had been built to provide shelter from storms and a way to get from one building to the other without going outside on winter days.

"I'll walk over with you," Zita said. "Does Sister Sharon want me to set up the coffee service for the meeting?"

We went downstairs, feeling our way in the dark by patting the walls. We groped our way past the art room and the costume room and past the little counter where one of the nuns used to sell religious items and school supplies and candy. We went into the tunnel. We could see light at the other end. The lights on the motherhouse side had not gone out.

Zita went up to the alumnae room. I went to Mother Celeste's room.

Sister Jeanette and Eddie Braddock were in the hall. "I understand you've gone ahead and contacted the Rosses," Eddie said.

"The nuns in this department have all been alerted," Sister Jeanette said. "We'll be ready at seven."

"I guess I can't persuade you to let an old woman die in peace," Eddie said. "I wash my hands of this. I'll see you tonight." He turned and walked away.

Sister Jeanette tapped on Mother Celeste's door and opened it. I went in. The rain was beating against the closed windows. The door to the porch, protected by the large overhang, was open. The wind was blowing in. Mother Celeste was sitting in a chair by the door. She was looking out at the storm.

"I asked Sister Jeanette to put me over here," she said. "This might be the last thunderstorm I'll ever see. Isn't it beautiful? Doesn't it smell wonderful? All my life, ever since I was a little girl, I've loved thunderstorms. Even tornadoes. A real Kansas girl. I'd always be the last one to go down in the storm cellar when I was a little girl. Frances, do you remember how the campus looked before the elm trees were cut down?"

"Yes, Mother." I didn't really, but I had seen pictures of the long drive when the trees on either side made a leafy tunnel from the motherhouse to the main gate.

"The maple trees are nice. Not like the elms, though. I hope the wind doesn't knock them down. They're beautiful when the leaves change. I won't see another autumn."

"The meeting is all arranged, Mother. I've talked to the Rosses, and Sister Sharon and Sister Jeanette are telling the nuns."

"I'm going to skip my medicine this afternoon so I'll be clear tonight if anyone wants to talk to me after the meeting."

"Any further instructions?"

"No, Frances. Just tell them I'm sorry. Tell them poor Sister Barbara did not take her own life. Ask them to forgive me and to pray for me. I've made so many mistakes." She was calm. There were no tears. She said nothing about murder.

I sat with her in silence for a while. We watched the storm, and at one point when the wind shifted, I got up and closed the door. After a while, Jeanette came in, and I left.

The lights had gone back on in the old convent. I went up to my room and lay down on the bed. I opened *Tom Playfair* and lost myself in the tale of a manly little lad of a century before.

At five, the sun came out. The campus, washed and fresh, looked like the paradise it must have been for the founders. I went outside. I walked down the long drive to the pergola. It was draped with wisteria. I thought of a picture I had seen once in an old *Crown* of academy girls in 1943 sitting here, lounging in chairs made of bent willow branches, reading letters from their boyfriends overseas. The chairs were gone. The girls were old women now. Some of the boys never came home.

The sadness of death hung over St. Adelaide's even as it gleamed refreshed in the sun. No students came to the academy anymore. No postulants came to the novitiate. The nuns who once had staffed the Adelaides' schools had left the order. They had come to find its ways as intolerable as the founders once had found the old German ways in Kentucky. There were no cows in the barnyard and no horses in the stable. There were no novices in the convent halls with their skirts pinned up and dust mops in their hands. The graveyard was full and the dormitories were empty. The superior of a dying order was spending her last days on earth making trouble. Why was she trying to hurt Sharon?

I walked over to the grotto. There were no goldfish in the moat. There were candles still in the dark cave and matches in the little safe. I lit all the candles. Please, Amma, Mother of us all, pray for me and for everyone who has knelt in this place. Spirits of all the nuns from all the orders from all the ages, spirits of all the boarding school girls from all the ages, protect my friend. Daddy, Mother, pray for me. *Omnes sanctae et sancti Deae, intercedite pro nobis.*

I walked out the main gate and headed uptown. The pickup trucks had left the square, and Harley's was empty. I went into Lucille's, the dress shop where St. Adelaide's girls once bought their uniforms. I was running out of clothes. I couldn't wear the yellow dress again.

Lucille had several dresses I liked, and I selected a black one. I asked her if she still had any old St. Ad's uniforms around. She found a blazer emblem in an old box of buttons. She gave it to me. It was a large *A*, embroidered in gold, with a crown above it and Queen Adelaide's motto scrolled below: *Aut vincam, aut periam.* Win, or die.

TEN

I TOOK A SHOWER downstairs and then went up to sit on the fire escape to dry my hair. I would wear the new dress. Since I wouldn't be presiding at the meeting, I wouldn't need my suit. It was too hot, anyway.

At six-thirty, Tom Ross drove up the long drive in a brown Chrysler and parked in front of the motherhouse.

Peter and Winnie Ross arrived at quarter to seven in their gray Rolls Royce. They parked behind their son's car. Peter Ross was wearing a khaki suit with a blue shirt and a rep tie. He had left his straw hat at home. He went around the car and helped Winnie out. She was in high heels again, darker than those she had been wearing earlier in the day. She had on a flowered dress and a dark jacket. They walked up the stone steps together.

At five minutes to seven, I went downstairs.

As I walked across the campus, Eddie Braddock drove up in his B.M.W., splashing through the puddles on the long drive.

We walked up the stone steps side by side. Eddie looked at me with disapproval, but kept his mouth shut. He was wearing a blue blazer now over the same outfit he had been wearing earlier in the day.

The nuns and the Rosses were in the alumnae room. The oldest nuns were in their wheelchairs by the French doors. Sister Jeanette and the other ambulatory nuns were in the wicker chairs in the front of the room. The Rosses were sitting by the refreshment table. Zita had put out a coffee urn, a plain one, not the silver one I remembered from school days. There were plates of cookies and a pitcher of punch. Zita was sitting at the back of the room by the rack of class pictures. I sat next to her.

Eddie Braddock went to the front of the room and stood by the little speaker's stand.

As the clock struck seven, Sharon came in from the serving room. She stood in front, apart from Eddie, and waited for quiet. Eddie Braddock looked at her and then at me. He was saying to me with his pudgy body language, "Come up here. You're being paid to conduct this meeting."

Sharon said, "Let us begin with a prayer. Come, Holy Spirit..."

Everyone joined in. At the end of the prayer, Eddie Braddock, still clinging to the speaker's stand, said, "With all due respect, Sister Sharon, my aunt had intended that Ms. Finn conduct this meeting."

Sharon said, "Mr. Braddock, in May, when Mother Celeste became so ill, the other members of the council and I assumed the direction of the community as our constitution requires. Because I was first councilor, assistant superior, I became acting superior. We haven't made this public yet because Mother Celeste finds it hard to accept, but we have informed the bishop. I preside over all our meetings now, and I will be presiding over this one. We will be discussing a matter that concerns only the Ross family and the community. For reasons of my own, I have asked Ms. Finn to remain." She waited, but Eddie did not leave.

He said, "You're trying to tell me that my aunt is no longer superior of St. Adelaide's? Absurd. I must insist that my aunt's wishes be carried out. She has hired Ms.

Finn to chair this meeting. I have signed a contract with Ms. Finn, engaging her services. I intend to see that she provides the services I am paying her to provide.''

"I'm sorry, Mr. Braddock. Our rule requires the assistant superior to take over when a superior is impaired by illness. Naturally, Mother Celeste's wishes are always of great importance to us, but this is out of her hands. It is the custom in our order to relieve the dying from temporal concerns so they can concentrate on spiritual matters.''

Eddie was up on tiptoes, clutching the reader's stand. "My aunt has said nothing to me about this. You intend to usurp her position?''

Sister Jeanette stood up and went to Eddie. She took his arm, and with her nurse's strength, led him out of the room. "Let me take you to Mother Celeste, Mr. Braddock. She's hoping you'll stop in to say good-night before you leave.'' His loafers could be heard tapping all the way down the hall.

Everyone seemed to exhale at once. The old nuns resumed fanning themselves with their Braddock Brothers Funeral Home fans. The Jesus pictured on the front suffering the little children was very Protestant looking.

Tom Ross stood up. "I'm not sure of the direction you intend to take, but my parents and I are prepared to...''

Peter Ross said in his loud, cruel voice, "Sit down, Tommy, and shut up!''

The old nuns stared. They liked hearing a contemporary of theirs deliver a sharp reprimand to a man only in his fifties, and a priest besides.

I was watching Sharon. She moved to the speaker's stand. She waited. When Sister Jeanette came back into the alumnae room, Sharon began speaking. "When Sister Barbara died in 1965, there was a different climate in religious life. We were afraid of the truth. It seemed more important to protect a good image than to tell the truth. I kept silence when I should have spoken.

"Mother Celeste has decided that she does not want to face judgment without setting out the facts of what happened to Sister Barbara. I agree with her that the time has come to tell the truth.

"I am going to speak plainly. Sister Barbara took an overdose of morphine the night before she died, probably before midnight. A doctor I have talked to tells me the drug would have acted on a body as slight as hers in about five hours, depending on the amount she ingested.

"I woke up early on the morning of December first. I slept in a little room off the freshman dorm, then, in the auditorium building. I got up and got dressed. I went over to the motherhouse. Something made me go to Sister Barbara's room to check on her. I had been with her in Guatemala, and I knew that she would often be very sick after a day of seeming to be better. The day before, she had visited with her parents and had gone to meals and recreation and prayers.

"She was occupying the corner room of the infirmary, the room Mother Celeste is in now. The infirmary was only three rooms then, not the whole southwest wing. I knew the minute I opened the door that she was dead. I put my hand under the cover, and there was a little warmth. In case there was a trace of life remaining, I said the Act of Contrition in her ear.

"There was a glass on the table by her bed, and there was a fruit jar that the morphine had been in. A doctor she went to in Guatemala had given her morphine. A big fruit jar full of pills. Barbara came back from the village to the mission one day with this big jar full of little silver pills. She started taking them all the time. I knew she was becoming addicted. I tried to get her to stop taking them. She got more pills from the doctor before we came home.

"When we got back to Braddock, she kept taking morphine. She said if she didn't take it, she got sick and threw up. She was so weak and so thin. Starved, almost. She couldn't eat. Sometimes she would try, but she couldn't.

"I put the scapular on her. I knew Our Lady would take Barbara to heaven. I knew Barbara wasn't in her right mind when she took the pills."

Tom Ross stood up. He walked toward Sharon. I was afraid he was going to strike her. He said, "You're a liar."

I wanted to protect her, but I didn't know how. I waited for his father to stop him, but Tom Ross continued, "You're going to stand here and tell us Barbara committed suicide? You would do this to my parents after all they have suffered? Barbara didn't kill herself. You killed her. That much I know. Barbara was planning to leave the convent. And you couldn't stand that. That would mean you wouldn't have your precious mission anymore. You'd go back to being the same ordinary little nothing you were before Guatemala. You'd spend your life as a freshman dorm prefect in a nothing little boarding school in the middle of nowhere. Instead of getting your picture in the paper for being a missionary, you'd be nothing. Another anonymous little nun in an anonymous little order no one ever heard of. If Barbara left the convent, you'd be nothing. You couldn't let Barbara leave. But she was determined to leave. You saw a solution to your problem. With Barbara dead, my family would keep on supporting the mission in Barbara's memory. You'd still have the prestige of being a missionary. You'd still get to wear a white habit and a missionary cross. You killed Barbara so you could go back to Guatemala. And when you killed Barbara, you killed *me*.''

There was saliva coming out of the corners of his mouth, but Sharon did not back away from him. She waited.

Peter Ross stood up and said, ''I told you to sit down and shut up. You're a fool, and you've always been a fool. You dare to stand up and embarrass me like this?''

Tommy sat down.

Sharon said, ''I didn't want anyone to know that Sister Barbara had committed suicide. It would have been horrible for the community. There would have been a police investigation or a coroner's investigation. I don't know what all. There were old nuns still alive then who would not have understood. We had a novitiate full of young sisters then. Please think back. There would have been a scandal. We still had the academy then, and we would have lost students if the girls' parents found out. The people in the town wouldn't have understood. It was a different world then. Everyone in this room can remember how sick Sister Barbara was. She wasn't responsible for what she did. Now, we would know how to help her. Then, we didn't. I took the jar the morphine had been in and the notes and went back over to the dorm.''

''*Notes!*''

Sharon opened a folder she had placed on a chair. ''Sister Barbara left five sealed envelopes on her desk. I took them that morning. I kept them. I have them here.

I never opened yours. Only my own." She handed envelopes to Winnie, Peter, Pauline, and Tom.

They stared at the letters from the past. "The letter Barbara left for me," Sharon said, "I opened that morning. It helped me decide to keep the truth from everyone. As you know, there were some in the community, particularly Barbara's classmates, who suspected all along that she had taken her own life."

The Rosses stared at the envelopes in their hands.

"Mother Celeste has been troubled about Sister Barbara's death. All these years she must have felt something was not right. She wanted to take care of it before she died. She asked Frances Finn, who is an experienced investigator, to come down here from Kansas City to help her reexamine the situation. When Frances told me what Mother had asked her to do, I realized it was time to tell what I knew.

"That's all I have to say. The Rosses would probably like to be left alone to read their letters. If any of the nuns have any questions, I'll be in the office after night prayer. I want to go report to Mother Celeste now." Sharon left the room.

Everyone sat in silence. Then Winnie started wailing. Her keening for her lost child filled the room. Her husband sat stiffly beside her, staring at the letter in his hand. Pauline got up and left the room.

Tom followed her.

One by one, the nuns left the alumnae room. When only Winnie and Peter were left, I decided to leave them alone with the truth of their daughter's death. I left the room and went downstairs. I went through the tunnel to the old convent. I didn't want to go the outside way in case Eddie or Tom or Pauline might be around. The meeting was over. The truth was told. It was only seven-thirty.

ELEVEN

WHEN I GOT UP to my room, I looked out the window. There on the grass below, Jack Braddock was leaning against the pillar that held the old convent bell.

I went downstairs and outside. "Am I late?"

"Not at all," he said. "I'm early. I couldn't wait to see you."

"Good. Let's get out of here."

Jack was driving one of the black Cadillacs. He opened the door for me and helped me in. He went around to the other side of the car and got in.

The Rosses' cars were still parked in front of the motherhouse.

Jack drove out the back gate. "You like my car?"

"Lovely. Funereal."

"I like your dress."

"Thank you. I got it today. At Lucille's."

"I want to show you something. Braddock's greatest tourist attraction." Jack turned up a country road. He drove along between corn fields for about a mile. He turned up a farm road. There, on a rise, was a farmhouse surrounded by trees. Behind it was a round barn. The barn rose three tiers from a stone foundation. Each tier was smaller in circumference than the one below it. The round barn was painted green and white and red.

"Incredible."

"It belongs to a friend of mine."

"It's incredible."

"The wood in that barn was salvaged from the St.

Louis World's Fair. Nineteen-oh-four. The lumber alone would cost half a million dollars today. That guy's grandfather built it. It had separate areas for everything, stalls for horses, a sheep pen, grain storage, milking area. Everything. The old man could turn a team of horses around in there. Places for his wagons and plows and tools. In that top little area was a place for the farm hands to bunk. When we were in high school, it was a ruin. They used it for a hay barn. We used to have make-out parties in there. Now this guy's restored it. My friend. Better than new.''

"Pauline Ross said something yesterday about barn restorations.''

"If you were going to be around for a few days, I'd show you the inside of the barn. We're not dressed for it now.'' Jack was wearing a blazer, white slacks, a beautiful tie. "The barn is immaculate inside, but we'd have to go across mud to get up there.''

"I've got to go home tomorrow. I'm sorry. I'd love to see the inside of that thing.''

"It's amazing. An architectural wonder. Original joists. It's been in magazines. Farm journals. Preservation magazines. You like the paint job?''

"It's your work.''

"Yes.''

"Beautiful.''

"That guy has tourists coming from all over the world to see the barn. A guy was here from Denmark the other day.''

"It must have cost a fortune to restore it to that condition.''

"My friend made some money when the interstate went through. Everybody made money on that. Even St. Ad's. Even me.''

"It's magnificent. The most beautiful barn I've ever seen."

Jack turned the car around, and headed back to the highway. "How's Mother Celeste?"

"She seemed good today. She was sitting up in a chair."

Jack lit a joint. He reached the highway and turned west. We drove toward the sun setting purple and orange behind the gathering storm clouds. The tension caused by the situation at St. Ad's and heightened by the terrible meeting in the alumnae room began to fall away. The limousine, the soft music, my handsome escort, the marijuana, the beautiful barn, the corn fields, all combined to make me feel happier than I had felt in months.

Jack sensed my joy and smiled at me. "How come you waited so long to come back to Braddock? Or have you been back, and I just didn't see you?"

"I swore on graduation day that I'd never come back."

"Why?"

"I don't know. I liked the girls at the academy. And I liked Braddock." The boy and the town. "But there was something about the nuns. Some of them didn't like me."

"Who didn't like you?"

"Mother Celeste, for one. She told me once that I looked like an unmade bed. And once she told me to get the supercilious look off my face."

"What does that mean?"

"Not good."

"So what made you come back now?"

"Mother Celeste wanted to talk to me. Do you know Sister Sharon?"

"Sure. She was my first grade teacher. I was in love with her. She was young. I think she was still a novice. Even though she wore a black veil. They sometimes had novices teach at St. George's. The ones close to making vows. For practice. She used to walk me back and forth from school. Holding my hand. I was a motherless child. My mom died when I was five."

"Mother Celeste had her get me down here."

"Why did you come down here in the first place? To school? Why didn't you go to high school in K.C.?"

"I was a motherless child, too. My mother died when I was nine. My dad was a private investigator. When I was ready to start high school, a guy my dad helped send to prison years before got out. The guy made some threats. I didn't know about it then. My dad just said he had to do some traveling for a very involved case he was working on. He might be in and out of town for months. Maybe even a year or two. He couldn't have me home by myself. He had heard about St. Adelaide's. He wrote to Mother Celeste. We came down here. I liked it. We decided that I'd come to school down here. After a year or two, the guy that had been making threats got killed. I could have stayed home then and gone to school in Kansas City, but by that time I was too involved with St. Ad's. I learned a lot at St. Ad's. Boarding school was good for me. Instead of being boy crazy in high school, I was book crazy. I had a serene adolescence. It turned out okay. Even though I didn't like the nuns, I liked boarding school."

Jack pulled into the country club parking lot. He pointed out a red Mercedes. "See that? My ex's car."

We walked around the pool and took a look at the tennis courts before going inside. Jack knew everyone and introduced me to several people. His former wife was sitting at the bar with two other women. She grabbed his hand as we passed. "Introduce us, Jack."

"Frances, I'd like you to meet Kathy Hermann. Kathy, this is Frances Finn."

We shook hands. Kathy was tiny and vivacious.

Jack and I went into the dining room. "Kathy looks like a cheerleader," I said.

"She was a cheerleader," he said. "Braddock and K.U. both. You don't remember her?"

We sat by the windows. A striped awning that covered the terrace outside the windows was flapping in the rising wind.

"Not really," I said. "When I was here, I didn't really look at the town girls that much. Only the boys."

"Remember the day we walked out to the turkey farm?"

"In the snow."

"I wondered if you remembered."

"I remember."

"I love that old road. No one ever goes out there. It's still the same. I go hunting out there sometimes. Walking, really. I carry a shotgun in case someone should see me and wonder what I'm doing. It's more macho to be hunting than just walking." Jack gave the waiter our drink order. Then he said, "I wasn't surprised when you walked into the station yesterday. I always knew I'd see you again."

We had cocktails and then ordered dinner. The storm rolled in, and the rain and lightning made a wonderful show. We talked about our work. I described a case I had just finished, and Jack talked about the gas station and the funeral home.

The dining room emptied out. We had dessert and

coffee. At one point, I asked, "Do you remember when Sister Barbara Ross died?"

"Sure. My dad figured she killed herself."

"He did?"

"Yeah. Pinpoint pupils. Other things he noticed. Morphine overdose."

"Your dad embalmed her?"

"Yes. What makes you think about her?"

"Pauline and I were talking about her last night."

"It was the talk of the town at the time. Dad never said anything. He figured the Rosses and the nuns wanted to keep it quiet. No point in giving the local gossips more grist for the mill. Lots of people you think die natural deaths really commit suicide. You learn that in the funeral business. Undertakers see it all the time. You'd be amazed at the number of people who commit suicide. I mention it in confidence about Sister Barbara."

"Your dad ran the funeral home?"

"Dan ran the funeral home, and Uncle Eddie was—is—president of the bank. Dad died in eighty-one. Now my brother Al runs the funeral home."

"And Eddie still runs the bank?"

"Eddie runs the bank when he's not on the golf course or playing bridge. He's got no kids, so I guess Al and I will inherit the bank. Maybe. Another thing you learn in the funeral business is don't count your chickens before they hatch. I'm not holding my breath."

"Do you play golf?"

"No. I hate golf. I hunt and fish. Walk around holding a shotgun, like I told you, or sit by a creek. The fish and game don't hide when they see old Jack coming. I paint houses and barns for people with taste. I

help my brother with funerals. I sit in the gas station. I
have lunch at the Rotary on Wednesdays. Other days, I
eat at Harley's. I eat dinner out here most nights. Sometimes I cook. I get my kids on weekends, and they only
live a block away anyway, so I see them all the time.
Kathy and I get along better than we did when we were
married. My life is sweet and easy. How about you?''

"Sweet and easy." It was strange to be discussing
life and death with a middle-aged man who was a
smooth-faced boy when I saw him last.

We went into the bar. Jack introduced me to Rudy
Cruz, the bartender. He poured cognac for us and put
on some oldies tapes. Jack and I danced for a while and
then left the country club. Jack drove along back roads
through the rain. Finally, he stopped the car on the turkey farm road. We sat in the car talking about our lives
and listening to the rain.

At one, we drove through the back gate to St. Adelaide's. Jack turned off the car lights to keep them from
shining in the chaplain's window. He turned off the
motor and let the car coast silently down the incline. As
we reached the old convent, lightning flashed, illumi-
nating the motherhouse. Someone was on the steps,
halfway down.

"Did you see that?"

"What?" Jack had been looking straight ahead.

"There's someone on the steps."

Jack started the car and turned the lights back on. He
turned the car to point the lights at the motherhouse.
No one was on the steps, and no car was parked in front.

TWELVE

THE BELL that woke me in the morning was not the big bell ringing the Angelus from the motherhouse dome. Instead, it was the old convent bell tolling from below. I jumped out of bed and ran to the window. Sharon was down there, pulling the rope. It was five-thirty. The old convent bell was rung only for the dead. It had tolled for Sister Barbara Ross on the day she died.

I put on my robe and ran down the stairs. Zita was coming out of her room, dressed in her habit as always. We went outside together and stood with Sharon as she tolled the bell. She said a Hail Mary between each stroke to time the slow knell. Ninety-four, ninety-five, ninety-six. It took nearly twenty minutes to ring the years of Mother's Celeste's life.

When she was finished at last, Sharon said, "Sister Jeanette went in to check on Mother at five o'clock. Mother wasn't in her bed. Jeanette couldn't figure out where she could possibly be. The door to the porch was open. Jeanette went out on the porch. Something made her look over the railing, and there was Mother on the ground below. Behind St. Adelaide. Jeanette ran down there, but Mother was dead. Cold."

Zita said, "Where is she now."

"Inside. On her bed. Father is there. He anointed her. Conditionally. He carried her inside. Jeanette ran to my room and got me as soon as she found Mother. I called Father, and he came right over. He carried her in and anointed her. I called the boys and the doctor and the nuns in Kansas City. The doctor came right out. She's with Mother now. She said Mother must have wandered out on the porch during the night. She must have had a heart attack. The doctor said she must have fallen against the railing and fallen over. She said she was probably dead before she hit the ground. It's terrible. It's unbelievable. The boys are on their way."

"What boys?" I asked.

"The Braddocks. Al and Jack. They're not boys. They're men. I don't know what I'm saying. I made a terrible mistake last night. I should never have gone ahead with the meeting. I was so angry. I've never been so angry in my life. I couldn't believe Mother would do such a thing. I wasn't thinking. I was worse than she was. Mother wasn't responsible for her actions. She was in so much pain, and she was so afraid of dying. She was just trying to hold onto the reins. After all these years, she couldn't let go. The whole thing was a way of being in control. It was just too much for her." Sharon was shaking, and her teeth were chattering.

Zita the undemonstrative put her arms around Sharon. "Come inside," she said.

"I can't," Sharon said. "I've got to get back."

I was about to tell her that I had seen Mother Celeste on the motherhouse steps the night before, but before I could say anything, Zita said, "Father's over there?"

"Yes. I've got to get back over there. It's terrible. If only I had handled last night better. I was so angry."

"Did you talk to her after the meeting?" I asked.

"Yes. I went in to tell her what I did. What I did when Barbara died and what I did at the meeting last night. I told her the whole story. Mother didn't seem upset at all. She said maybe it was for the best. She told me she was sorry for all the trouble she was causing me. She told me she knew Barbara wouldn't have killed herself without leaving a note, and she certainly wouldn't have taken an overdose of pills and then put her scapular on. Mother told me she was sorry. She said with her particular judgment coming, she had to do something. She said she's been trying to figure it out all these years. It's unbelievable.'' Sharon started crying. ''Now her particular judgment is over.''

Zita led her up to the porch of the old convent. ''Just come in here for a minute. You're going to have a long day.'' She led her into the infirmary. She put a shawl over Sharon's shoulders and guided her to the chair.

Sharon huddled in the black shawl. She looked old to me for the first time.

Zita had filled the tea kettle and put it on the hot plate before going outside. Now she put tea bags in three cups. She poured the boiling water.

''Did the Rosses go in to see Mother?'' I asked.

''They all went in. One by one. I think Mother was so upset after talking to them, that she couldn't sleep. She hadn't taken her medicine all day. She wanted to be alert. The shock was too much for her. I'll never forgive myself. I should have told her what I was going to do. I was too angry. She got you down here, Frances, and led you to believe that she thought I murdered Barbara Ross. She didn't really think that. It's just that she's been so furious at me since May. She hatched this little scheme to get even with me for taking over the direction of the community. She told me at the time that she'd get even with me. She always exaggerated everything so much. Histrionic. Always an actress. I took it with a grain of salt. When she told me to get you down here, it never occurred to me that she was using you to get at me. She knew we were friends. She dreamed up this scheme about Sister Barbara's death to get even with me. It backfired.''

Zita said, "Father anointed her?"

"Yes. Jeanette's with her. And Father. And several of the nuns woke up when they heard the commotion. They'll all be awake now. After hearing the bell. They'll all be with her." Sharon started crying again.

Zita put a cup of tea on the table by Sharon. "What about Ed Braddock?" she asked.

"I couldn't reach him," Sharon said. "Al and Jack said they'd let him know. I've got to get back over there. I don't know what to do. I've got to make a list. I don't know if we can have the office of the dead on Sunday, or what. I don't know what to do about the funeral."

"Why?" I asked. "What's the problem with the funeral?"

"Mother had a thing about recycling. She read a thing about ecologically correct funerals, and that's what she wanted. She had Al Braddock out here after her surgery to tell him what she wanted. Immediate burial, no laying out, no embalming, no coffin. Just a cardboard box. He agreed to do it."

"So what's the problem?"

"The nuns will want a funeral. People will want to come. Alumnae from all over the country."

"You don't need a body," I said. "Bury her today, if that's what she wanted. Then have a memorial service when everybody gets here."

Zita handed me a cup of tea. Then she sat down on the other chair, and faced Sharon. She said, "You've got lots of people to help you get through today and the next few days. People with experience. Sister Jeanette. Father. Even me. The Braddocks. Frances here. We don't want you to get sick. Stop thinking about last night. It's over. Drink your tea. Then I'll walk over with you. The first thing we have to decide is, what time is mass going to be?"

Mass was at eight on ordinary Sundays. Sharon said, "I don't know. I don't know if we can have a requiem on Sundays, or what."

Zita said, "We'll make a list. Drink your tea." We sat in silence for a few minutes. Then Zita said, "I've got to get over there and see what Father wants to do. He has to eat breakfast." The two of them got up and left the room together. Sharon carried her cup with her. Zita's side rosary rattled as they walked down the hall.

I took a shower and went upstairs. I dressed in slacks and a blouse.

As I walked across the campus to the motherhouse, Jack Braddock drove up the long drive in the hearse. He and another man got out. Jack said, "Frances, this is my brother Al. Al, this is Frances Finn." Al looked like Jack. Both looked like Burt Lancaster in *From Here to Eternity*. Strong, beautiful men.

Al Braddock and I shook hands. "I'm sorry for your loss," I said.

Al said, "Mother Celeste had a long, full life. I'm glad her suffering is over."

We went inside. Sharon and Jeanette and the chaplain were in the rotunda. Sharon hugged Jack and then Al. She said, "Thank you for coming." The grandfather clock struck seven. "Should we ring the Angelus?" she asked.

"Not until Mother is buried," Sister Jeanette said. She was composed as nurses are in the face of death. "Until then we'll use the clacker." An old nun sitting nearby in her wheelchair volunteered to go to the sacristy to find the clacker.

Al and Jack shook hands with the chaplain and with the various nuns who were passing through the rotunda on their way to Mother Celeste's room. Sharon led them to their great-aunt's room. I followed. She explained to them in a soft voice what had happened.

Mother Celeste lay on her bed, covered up to her shoulders. Two candles burned by her bed. Her face was discolored. Her hair was wet and dark with blood. There was a deep wound above her right ear, and her mouth was slightly open, showing her perfect teeth one last ghastly time.

The door and windows were open to the cool morning. Several nuns were in the room. Some were kneeling. A few were standing. Others, in wheelchairs, were in the hall outside the door. They were praying silently. Jack and Al knelt down by Mother Celeste's bed. They took rosaries from their pockets and crossed themselves. I knelt beside them. The doctor, a stout, gray-haired woman, was sitting in the chair by the door writing in a little notebook. After a few minutes, I got up and left the room.

Sharon was in the office. "I'm calling the nuns in St. Louis," she said. "Wait for me in the parlor. I'll be right there."

I sat down in the front parlor on the same Victorian loveseat I had sat on with my dad when we came to enroll at St. Ad's. Thirty years had gone by. Mother Celeste had seemed old to me then, and now she was dead. She had given me my laundry number, seventeen, and told me where to buy my uniforms, uptown at Lucille's.

Al and Jack came into the room. They were discussing the ecologically correct funeral. Al said, "I've got one of those boxes that she wanted, but people aren't going to like the looks of it."

Sharon came into the room. She said, "I've called the nuns in Kansas City, St. Louis, and San Antonio. They're going to call everyone else as soon as I call them back with details. They'll put the notice in the papers. I've just now talked to the other councilors, and they're going to call the bishop. They want me to ask you what you think about Mother's idea for a funeral."

Al said, "My policy is to do what people want, ordinarily. But Mother Celeste was a public figure, and people will want to see the body. They'll need time to get here. They'll expect a wake. I think what you should have is a big funeral. This is the end of an era, not just of one old lady's life. I tried to explain that to Mother Celeste last month, but you know how she is. Was."

Jack said, "It's going to be in the nineties today. We've got to embalm her or bury her. I can get a kid out here this morning with a gravedigger, but I don't think folks are going to like it. I think Al is right."

"And Ed will want a big funeral. You can bet your life on that," Al said.

Sharon sat down. "Mother would be furious if she heard this conversation. She would want us to do exactly what she wanted us to do. She was so specific about it."

Jeanette came in. "Excuse me, Sister Sharon," she said. "The doctor is leaving. She wants to make sure you're feeling all right."

"I'm fine," Sharon said.

Jeanette said, "Have you decided about Mother? If we're going to keep her here without embalming her,

I'll wash her now, and dress her. She wanted to be buried in the old habit. I've got everything ready.''

The discussion about embalming versus natural burial went on. The doctor came into the room and joined the discussion. She said, ''I called the police on my way out here. Chief Hermann should be here any minute.''

Jack said, ''You called Randy Hermann?''

The doctor said, ''We need a police report when there's an accident.''

''What accident?'' Al said. ''I thought you said she had a heart attack before she went over the railing.''

''That's right, but I have to do things by the book. I just want Randy to take a look.'' She turned to Sharon. ''I'll be going now, Sister,'' she said.

Sharon and Jeanette walked to the door with the doctor. Al Braddock followed them. Jack said to me, ''Will you be sticking around for the funeral?''

''I doubt it. Unless they go ahead with the instant burial today.''

''They won't. Take my word for it. The bishop isn't going to want a hurry-up funeral. Mother Celeste was the mother superior here for sixty years. A big shot. Therefore, a big funeral. With the bishop as the center of attention. Every priest in the diocese will be here. Priests from other dioceses. Nuns from other orders. Alumnae from all over the place. The bishop will be the star of the show. He won't pass this up. He'll tell the nuns to take their time. And Uncle Eddie as the chief mourner? He'll need time. I'd say the funeral will be Wednesday.''

''Jack, do you remember when I saw someone on the steps last night?''

''Yes.''

''It must have been Mother Celeste.''

"I thought they said she fell over the railing."

"That's what they think, but I think she walked down the steps. She must have walked down the steps, and then walked around there behind the statue."

"She could never walk down those steps. In the pouring rain. When I saw her a month ago, she could barely move."

"She was sitting up in a chair yesterday."

"There's no way in hell she could have walked down those steps."

"Then who was that on the steps?"

Al came back into the parlor. "Randy's here," he said. "Sister Sharon's showing him where they found the body."

We looked out the window. We could see the police car parked in front, but the wide porch blocked our view of Sharon and Chief Hermann below. Jeanette came into the parlor. "Any decisions?" she asked.

"Not yet," Al said.

I said, "Sister, are you sure Mother fell over the railing?"

"What do you mean?"

"I mean, could she have walked down the steps and gone around to where you found her?"

"No. She had been walking from her bed to her chair and back a couple of times a day. But I had to hold her. She couldn't have gone that far by herself. I'd say she wanted a closer look at the storm. She went out on the porch. Then she had a heart attack. The surge of pain pitched her over the railing."

"How did she get that gash on her head?" Jack asked.

"Hit her head on the pavement, I suppose. I guess

she went down head first. I just hope the doctor's right, that Mother didn't suffer.''

Sharon and Chief Hermann came up the steps. We watched them walk along the porch to the place where Mother Celeste was presumed to have gone over. Randy Hermann was an energetic man, slim, dressed in plain clothes. He looked like his sister, the cheerleader. He leaned over the railing and looked down. He nodded to Sharon, and they went into Mother Celeste's room through the door to the porch.

After a while, they came into the parlor. Jack introduced us. Chief Hermann did not seem surprised to find a private investigator from Kansas City in the convent parlor at seven-thirty in the morning. He made some notes in his notebook. Then he said to Sharon, ''That's about it, Sister. Routine. My guess is that death came before the accident. I'd say the doctor's right. Mother Celeste had a heart attack and fell over the railing. She was dead before she hit the ground. Natural death. You can let Al here take the body. I'm going to put down that there was no accident. Too bad she had to end up in a puddle on the sidewalk, but sometimes these things happen.''

Sharon invited the police chief to stay for breakfast, but he declined. Sharon walked with him to the front door. She came back to the parlor, but before she could speak, Sister Jeanette came to the doorway and said, ''Sister Sharon, the bishop is on the phone. He wants to talk to you.''

Sharon hurried away. Al said, ''I'll go move the hearse to the south door.''

The old nun who had gotten the clacker from the sacristy was sitting in her wheelchair in the rotunda, ready to sound it. A few nuns were going past her into the chapel.

Sharon came back from the office. "The bishop wants the funeral to be on Wednesday. No cardboard boxes."

"We'll take care of everything," Jack said. He left the room. Sharon and I waited in the parlor until we heard the elevator door open. Jack and Al rolled a stretcher across the rotunda and down the hall to Mother Celeste's room.

Sharon nodded to the old nun in the wheelchair. She began sounding the clacker. One slow knock followed another. The nuns who had been in the chapel came out. Others appeared from their rooms in the infirmary. The kitchen sisters came up from the ground floor. The nuns arranged themselves around the rotunda and down the hall as Al and Jack wheeled Mother Celeste's body to the elevator. Her face was covered now. The chaplain followed. He sprinkled the corpse with holy water, and some of the nuns cried as their superior's body passed. After the elevator door closed, several of the nuns went out on the porch to watch Jack and Al load the body into the hearse at the south door below. Jeanette and Sharon got into a convent car and followed the hearse down the long drive.

The nuns and the chaplain went inside. I followed. Zita was in the rotunda. She said to the chaplain, "Will you be coming back to your house, Father?"

"Not until after mass, Sister. Don't worry about me. I'll eat breakfast in the refectory."

As the nuns went into the chapel, Zita signaled to me to follow her.

THIRTEEN

WE WENT OUTSIDE, and crossed the lilac field to the chaplain's house. In the kitchen, Zita lit the stove, pinned up her sleeves, and put on a gingham apron. She plugged in the coffee maker and took two brown eggs from a bowl. "Scrambled or poached?"

"Poached, please."

"Baker's bread or convent bread?"

"Convent bread, please."

As she squeezed oranges, Zita said, "I don't think Mother Celeste fell over the railing at all. How could she possibly have gotten out of bed, gone over to the door, out the door, and across the porch in the pouring rain? She couldn't get from her bed to the chair without Sister Jeanette practically carrying her. And why didn't she put her robe on? And even if she managed to get to the railing, and then had a heart attack, why wouldn't she just fall where she was? On the porch. She wouldn't have gone over the railing. Mother was short. That railing would have been up to her waist. Higher. I think she was pushed over. Or dropped over. Or thrown over. I think Mother Celeste was murdered."

All this was said in a conversational tone. Zita poured the orange juice into a glass. Then she broke eggs into a little poacher. She continued, "Last night I was halfway waiting up for you. I couldn't sleep after the meeting. I just kept thinking about Sister Barbara. I always knew Sister Barbara killed herself. I just knew it. I couldn't sleep, so I got up. I thought I might as well take some stuff over to the laundry. Father's towels and stuff. It was already Sunday, technically, and I don't usually go to the laundry on Sundays, but it was more like Saturday night still. It was after midnight. Almost one. I figured if you came back while I was over there, you'd get in okay. You had your key, right? I went through the tunnel. I was walking by the trunk room, and all of a sudden I got a notion to go in there and take a look in Sister Barbara's trunk. I never thought to look in her trunk before. I went in there, and you know how those little basement windows look out under the porch? Those little windows are in the trunk room. Were you ever in there? It's where the nuns' trunks are kept. I was standing in there in the dark, feeling around for the light string. All of a sudden, it lightninged a huge flash of lightning. It lit up the front steps. There was somebody out there. Going down the steps."

Zita arranged a place setting on the little table. She placed my orange juice in front of me.

"Who was it?"

"I don't know."

"Man or woman?"

"I couldn't tell. It happened too fast. The lightning flashed, and I saw feet on the steps. Going down. It was like an afterimage, really. I can't say what kind of feet. I was half blinded by the lightning, and it didn't register immediately."

"Did they see you?" The feet? What was I talking about?

Zita poured coffee for me. She put butter and marmalade in front of me. She arranged the toasted convent bread and the eggs on a plate. She put the plate in front of me. "No, I never turned on the light." She looked

out the window. It was starting to rain again. "Happy
the corpse the rain falls on," she said.

Just then, Eddie Braddock drove past. He parked in
front of the motherhouse, got out of his car, locked the
door, and ran up the steps to the main entrance.

"Did you go to the laundry then?" I asked.

"No. I was too scared. I thought it was a bum. You
know how bums used to come around here all the time?
For food. A little work. They don't come anymore.
They used to ride the Katy Flyer. Jump off before they
got too close to Kansas City. They knew they could
always get a meal at the convent. And that I'd give them
some work in the barn. They were willing to do a little
work for a meal. I wasn't afraid of them. They were
just men that never got readjusted after the war. You
can't train somebody to be a killer and then expect them
to readjust. I guess I was thinking about that. Times are
different now. Bums are different. I didn't feel like un-
locking the south door and going outside. It was pouring
down rain and lightning, anyway. And with somebody
sneaking around outside, I just decided to go back and
go to bed. Next thing I knew, I heard the bell outside.
At first I kept on dreaming. I thought it was years ago
when you kids were in school, and Jack Braddock and
his no-good friends were out there ringing that bell. Remember that? I was dreaming they were out there ringing the bell. Then I woke up, and the bell really was
ringing, only it was Sister Sharon ringing it, and I knew
Mother was dead."

"What kind of shoes?"

"I can't remember."

"Feet are very distinctive. People in Muslim countries where they wear robes and turbans and face veils
can recognize each other by their feet."

"I'm trying to think, but it was so quick."

"Close your eyes. Picture how it looked."

Zita closed her eyes. She concentrated. "It's like a negative. I can picture it, but I can't tell anything."

"You're sure the person was going down, not up?"

"Yes."

"I saw the person, too."

"What do you mean?"

"Jack and I had just driven in. He drove in the back way, and just before he got to the house here, he turned off the car lights and the motor. He didn't want the lights to shine in and wake up Father. He coasted down to the old convent. I was looking at Jack, and over his shoulder, I saw someone on the motherhouse steps when the lightning flashed. It must have been exactly the same time you were in the basement over there."

"Who was it?"

"I couldn't tell, either. Jack turned the car around to shine the lights over there, but by then, the person was gone. And there was no car parked outside. I didn't think anything of it. This morning, when I heard what happened, I figured it was Mother Celeste."

"It wasn't Mother Celeste."

"How do you know?"

"The feet were in the middle of the steps. The person was walking down the middle. Mother Celeste, even if she could have gone down those steps, would have been at the side, holding on to the banister."

"That's right." I closed my eyes and recalled the image I had seen. The person in my own mental negative was in the middle also.

"Was yours a man or a woman?"

I closed my eyes again. "I couldn't tell," I said. It

was just a dark form visible in the flash of lightning against the lighter steps.

Through the window, we saw Eddie Braddock run down the steps, unlock his car, get in, and drive fast down the long drive.

"Did you ever look in Barbara's trunk?" I asked.

"No. I'll go over there sometime and take a look. I don't know if her trunk's still there or not. No one ever goes in there. The meat lockers are down there, and since we stopped butchering, we don't use those. There are trunks in there of nuns who died eighty years ago."

"I'm surprised the antique dealers didn't take them."

"They mostly bought the stuff in the old convent. Mother wanted to sell stuff in the motherhouse, but some of the nuns talked her out of it."

"So who was that on the steps, and what was he doing? Or she."

"I think someone killed Mother Celeste," Zita said. "All that talk from Sharon this morning. About murder. What was that all about?"

I explained to Zita what Mother Celeste had wanted me to do.

Zita snorted. She poured more coffee for me. She sat down across from me with her own coffee. "Mother Celeste never thought Barbara Ross was murdered. Or that Sharon murdered her. She knew what happened. I saw Mother Celeste *and* Sister Sharon that morning."

Somehow I wasn't surprised. Zita was always walking around in the middle of the night. She had her own timetable, unrelated to anyone else's.

She said, "The day before Sister Barbara died, I waited on her and her parents at table. They ate dinner in the girls' dining room. About one in the afternoon. The girls had already finished and left. Only Sister Barbara and her parents were in there. We always gave them better food than any other guests. Mother Celeste always wanted them to have the best.

"I was going back and forth from the kitchen to the dining room. I could hear them talking. Sister Barbara was begging her parents to take her home. To let her come home. She was crying. Her parents were embarrassed. They were trying to make her shut up so I wouldn't hear her.

"Sister Barbara was always unhappy in the convent. I could see that from the day she entered. I was a second-year novice when Barbara Ross entered. She wasn't the type for the convent. She liked to make her own decisions. She was a good girl, but she wasn't meant to be a nun. I always liked her. I liked her when she was in school, and I liked her after she entered. The kitchen sisters always liked her, too. She always helped. She always went straight out to the kitchen after meals. The other nuns would rush off to recreation or back over to the academy after supper, but Barbara always went straight out to the kitchen. She would do the dirty work, too. Scrub pots. Scour those big pans from the steam table. She never thought she was too good for hard work. But she was unhappy.

"She was crying that day. The day before she died. Her parents brought her presents like they always did. Boxes of food. Caviar and stuff like that. Avocados. Stuff the other nuns never got. She would give it away as soon as they left. She never ate that stuff. She would give the caviar to the kitchen sisters when her parents left. She would give me the avocados. She gave everything away, always. At Christmas, when she was teaching at St. George's, she would always get a big bunch of presents from the kids. Handkerchiefs, talcum powder. The kind of stuff kids used to give the nuns. She would bring it all home, still wrapped. She had me help her. We would take off the little tags and put new ones on for the old nuns. That way, on Christmas morning, all the old nuns who didn't get presents anymore because their families were dead or something would get presents. They didn't know who they were from. We just wrote 'from Santa' on the tags. The nuns would be so happy. They would show the presents to each other and try to guess where they came from.

"Anyway, that day, her parents told her they wouldn't take her home. They said she was sick. That she needed to see a psychiatrist.

"I was worried about her. The next morning early, I decided to go over and see if she was okay. I was trying to be quiet, because I didn't want to wake anybody up. I started down the hall, and then I saw Mother Celeste coming down those stairs at the end of the hall. She lived on the second floor then, right above where she lives now. Lived. She didn't see me. There was only a real dim light in that hall at night. I stepped back into a parlor doorway so she wouldn't see me. She got about halfway down the stairs, and then she turned and went back up. I started to go back over to the academy, but then I heard Sister Sharon coming down the hall. Mother Celeste must have heard her coming. That's why she went back upstairs. Sharon went past me. She didn't see me. I didn't say anything. She went down to Sister Barbara's room. She opened the door. I saw the light go on in there. Then I saw Mother Celeste come a little way down the stairs again. She must have been able to see in the room through the transom. Well, I know she could, because later I tried it. From that place where she was standing on the stairs, she could see into the room. After a while, Sharon came out. She was carrying some stuff. The letters and the jar and the glass. I didn't know that was what it was though, at the time. She turned off the light in Sister Barbara's room, and closed the door. Mother Celeste didn't say anything to her. If Sharon had turned around, she would have seen Mother Celeste on the stairs.

"I waited in the parlor for a long time. Finally, the rising bell rang, and I went over to the laundry. Later, when they told me Sister Barbara was dead, I wondered what Sharon was doing. When I heard Barbara had her scapular on, I figured Sharon had put it on her. I figured Barbara had killed herself, and Sharon had done what she could to cover it up. I had it pretty much figured out like Sharon told us last night. I don't understand why Mother Celeste would twist it all around and talk about murder. Sometimes old people do that. They get mean at the end. It's like they've been nice on the outside all along, but the way they really are on the inside comes out at the end. It's like a doctor I used to work for in Kansas City. I did everything for him. For years. He bragged on me to everyone. In those days, in Kansas City, in our neighborhood at least, doctors still had their offices in their houses. This one did. On Armour Boulevard. I was his nurse, secretary, chief cook and bottle washer. Then, right before he died, he started accusing me of stealing from him. No one took him seriously. His wife told me not to worry. She knew he was just losing his mind. She knew I didn't steal anything from him. She paid my dowry when I entered the convent. I'm just saying that people who are dying sometimes die bit by bit, and the brain goes first.

"Mother Celeste was always jealous of Sister Sharon. Mother Celeste was the jealous type. The academy girls always liked Sharon better than Mother Celeste. You did too, didn't you? I think Mother Celeste decided to get you down here to help her pull one last mean trick on Sharon. To get even with Sharon for taking over the community. You'd be the perfect one. She knew you and Sharon were friends, that you still get together in Kansas City. You'd be the perfect one to help her get back at Sharon. Mother Celeste always had a mean streak. She was mad at Sharon for taking over the community in May. Poor Sharon. You know her heart is bad?''

"I hope the strain of this doesn't kill her," I said.

Zita poured more coffee in our cups. She took away my plate. She said, "I think Sharon would be better off knowing someone else killed Mother Celeste. As it is, she'll blame herself. She'll go on thinking Mother was upset about the meeting and fell over the railing."

"It wasn't Sharon's fault," I said. "It's ironic that Mother Celeste herself would be murdered after trying to accuse someone else of murder. Poetic justice."

"You should investigate."

"Investigate what?"

"Find out who that was on the steps. That person was the murderer."

"Investigating means asking questions. No one's going to answer my questions. What if I went up to Tom Ross and said, 'Just out of curiosity, I'm wondering if you snuck into Mother Celeste's bedroom, carried her out on the porch, and dropped her fifteen feet to the sidewalk'? He might get mad. You saw how he was last night. I'd be too scared if he came at me like he did to Sharon. I was afraid he was going to slug her. I've got to get home. I'm running out of clothes."

"You're not staying for the funeral?" The phone

rang. Zita answered. "Chaplain's residence...yes, I
have one...yes, she's here with me...we'll bring it."
She hung up, and said to me, "That was Sharon.
They're at Braddock Brothers. They need a liner...the
short veil we wear under our long veils. Sister Jeanette
forgot to pack one for Mother. I told them I'd bring one
if you'll drive me uptown. Or I can walk if you're in
such a big hurry to get home."

I said, "Let's talk to Sharon and Jeanette. See what
they say. We'll see if they want to investigate."

We washed the dishes and walked back to the old
convent. Zita opened a drawer in her room and took out
a short black veil. She said, "This was my profession
liner. I wear it on Christmas."

FOURTEEN

JACK WAS STANDING in the parking lot at the funeral home. Eddie Braddock's B.M.W. was parked next to the hearse and the limousines. Jack opened the door of my car and helped Sister Zita out. He said, "Sister Sharon isn't feeling too well. She's lying down inside. I've suggested to Sister Jeanette that she take Sister Sharon back to the convent and put her to bed. Al and I can take care of the body."

Zita said, "We always wash and dress the sister ourselves."

Jack said, "I know, Sister. Would you want to stay here and dress Mother Celeste? Al and I will help. Mother Celeste was our aunt, you know. It's not like strangers doing it."

We went inside. Sharon was in the front parlor lying on a couch by the window. I saw Peter Ross, across the street, come out on his porch in his robe and slippers. He picked up the *Kansas City Journal-Post* from the walk and went back inside.

Sharon said she was feeling a little weak. Jeanette and Zita conferred for a short time with Al and Jack. They decided that Jeanette would drive Sharon back to the convent, and Zita would remain to help prepare Mother Celeste's body. I offered to stay with her and then drive her back to St. Adelaide's. "It shouldn't take more than two hours," Al Braddock said.

Sharon and Jeanette left. Zita went downstairs with Al to the preparation room, and I went into the kitchen with Jack. "Have you had breakfast?" he asked. "Eddie went for doughnuts. Making himself useful for a change."

"Sister Zita fed me. Thanks."

"Coffee?"

"Please."

Jack poured a cup of coffee for each of us and sat down with me at the table. The large kitchen was beautifully decorated with blue and white tiles and pottery.

"This place is fabulous," I said.

"Thanks. After I got divorced, I moved back here with my brother. He never married. We both like painting and woodworking. My dad was the same way. House proud. All the Braddocks are house proud. The place was in good condition, but Al and I decided to bring it up to date."

"Jack, Sister Zita saw that person on the steps last night, too."

"Who was it?"

"She couldn't tell. She was in the motherhouse, in the basement, after midnight. Just about the time we were driving in. The nuns' trunk room is down there, right under the front steps. Zita was in there, and when the lightning flashed, she saw the person on the steps. Through the little basement window. Just for a split second. Just the feet."

"Man or woman?"

"She couldn't tell."

"It must have been Mother Celeste. We should have gone over there and looked around. We might have found her in time to do something. I wasn't thinking. Maybe we could have done something."

"Jack, it couldn't have been Mother Celeste. The person was in the middle of the steps. Not holding on to the banister. Mother Celeste could never have gone down those steps without holding on."

"So who was it?"

"Zita thinks someone pushed Mother Celeste over the railing. Or even carried her to the railing and dropped her over."

Jack stared at me for a long time. Finally he asked, "Do you think that, too?"

"It could be."

"Why would anybody want to kill a little old lady that's about to die any minute anyway?"

"There was a meeting last night at the convent. That's why Mother Celeste had me come down here. She wanted me to conduct a meeting with the nuns and some other people. There were some very hard feelings by the time it was over. I'm not sure just what went on after I left with you, but I wouldn't be surprised at anything."

"The Rosses."

"Right."

"I saw their cars." He looked at me again for a long time. Then he said, "Mother Celeste's body is really broken up."

"It is?"

"Her shoulder is broken. That much we can tell. Without an autopsy, we can't tell too much, but we think her right leg is broken, too. There's a big gash in the side of her head. I guess you saw that. The hair is all pushed in there."

"What does your brother say?"

"Nothing. He just says the broken bones are consistent with an old person falling fifteen feet onto concrete. The arms aren't broken."

"What does that mean?"

"I don't know. Nothing, maybe. Maybe that she didn't try to stop herself from falling. That she was dead before she went over the railing. Like the doctor said. That's what I hope."

"What do you think should be done?"

"You mean like an autopsy?"

"Yes."

"If we say anything, it will mean an autopsy and an official investigation. It will mean a lot of bad publicity for the Adelaides and a lot of stress and strain on Sister Sharon. It means my ex-brother-in-law will be out there asking questions. Does Sharon know about the person on the steps?"

The door to the kitchen opened, and Eddie Braddock came in. He put his umbrella on the floor and said, "The word is all over town already. People are wondering how the nuns could leave a sick old lady alone like that. Let her wander off and fall off the porch. When she wasn't in her right mind anyway."

"Big crowd in the doughnut shack, Eddie?" Jack asked.

"The situation at St. Adelaide's is out of control," Eddie said. "Sister Sharon suddenly decides *she's* the superior. Then she drags in outsiders to meddle…"

Jack said, "Frances, I believe you've met my Uncle Ed?" He picked up the dripping umbrella and put it outside the door.

"We've met," Eddie said. "I would have thought you'd be back in Kansas City by now, Ms. Finn. Surely your work here is finished."

"I've decided to stay for the funeral," I said.

Sister Zita came into the kitchen. She said, "Al doesn't need me for about an hour."

I said, "Do you want to go to St. Ad's, and then come back?"

"No, I'll wait. If that's all right with you, Jack."

"Of course. Coffee? Doughnut?"

"No, thank you."

Eddie poured coffee for himself, and sat down at the breakfast table. He opened the newspaper and started eating a doughnut.

Jack led Zita and me out of the kitchen. We passed through a butler's pantry and went into the dining room. Beyond the dining room was a large parlor, apparently the one used for wakes. Jack took us in there and closed the doors. He said, "Sister Zita, Frances told me what you saw last night. It looks to me like Mother Celeste's death needs some looking into. Somebody was sneaking around the convent at one o'clock in the morning in the middle of a thunderstorm. Just about the time my great-aunt went over the railing. I don't like the idea of somebody killing a helpless old woman, a nun, one of my relatives, and thinking he can get away with it. I'd like to find out who was on the convent steps last night. I want to know who killed my aunt. And I want to know why."

"Are you going to call the police?" Zita asked.

"The police is Randy Hermann. He's not exactly Sherlock Holmes. I don't want him out there bothering Sister Sharon. I don't want the funeral held up by an autopsy. I just think we need a discreet investigation. A few questions put to a few people. Done with finesse. Frances? Can you think of a way to look into this without drawing too much publicity to the convent? If you can, and if you're willing to take it on, I'd like to hire you."

"Without telling Randy Hermann?"

"Exactly."

Zita asked me, "Have you told Jack about the meeting?"

"Not everything. Jack knows there was a meeting. He knows who was there. But I haven't told him the topic of discussion."

"Barbara Ross's death would be my guess," Jack said.

"That's right," I said.

"Do you think one of the Rosses killed my aunt?"

"I don't know. It got pretty tense last night."

"Would you be willing to investigate?"

"I would, Jack. I should tell you that I don't know if I can find out anything. I haven't had any experience in this kind of thing."

"Murder."

"Right. I'd hate to screw it up. I might ask the wrong person the wrong question, and instead of finding out anything, end up warning that person to be more careful. And even if I ask the right questions, I can't guarantee that anybody will talk to me."

"Tell them I've hired you to look into Mother Celeste's death. If somebody refuses to answer your questions, that tells us something right there, doesn't it?"

"What about Eddie?" I asked.

"He's not going to like it. Tough. I don't like it that somebody killed a helpless old nun. I don't care about offending people. Anyway, nobody's going to be offended except the murderer."

"That's what I mean."

"You think Eddie did it?"

"Would he have a motive?"

"Maybe. He wasn't at the meeting, was he?"

"No. Sister Sharon more or less asked him to leave before it started."

"I saw him driving out the gate when I was driving in. That doesn't mean he didn't go back."

"Your uncle doesn't know what went on at the meeting, Jack," Zita said. "It's something that could hurt the convent's reputation."

"Worse than the mother superior getting murdered?"

Zita and I told Jack about the meeting. I told him everything, including Mother Celeste's original intent to make people think Sister Barbara Ross had been murdered. I told Jack and Zita about my meeting with Tom Ross and his accusation of Sharon.

Al Braddock came into the room. He said, "Sister Zita, we can dress Mother Celeste now and casket her. If you're ready."

Zita went with him. Jack said, "I'm going to have to tell my brother about this. He'll want to go in with me on hiring you."

Through the window, we saw Pauline Ross drive up to her parents' house and park her car. She went inside. After a few minutes, she came out again and crossed the street. She came up the walk to the funeral home. Jack went to the front hall and let her in.

"Jack," she said. "My parents called me. I'm very sorry to hear about Mother Celeste."

"Thank you, Pauline."

They came into the parlor. "Frances, you're here?"

"I drove Zita uptown."

"I'm going to put out a special edition," Pauline said. "I can't wait for Saturday for this. The death of a person whose life encapsulates the entire history of the Adelaide order in Kansas, who started out in the minim class in nineteen-oh-one, and ended up as mother superior. When's the funeral?''

"Wednesday," Jack said.

"I'll put out the special on Tuesday. That way it'll be ready for the funeral. I've got to get out to the convent and get some pictures. The body is here now?''

"We'll be taking her back out when Al and Sister Zita are finished downstairs," Jack said.

"She had a heart attack?"

"That's what the doctor said."

"And fell over the railing?"

"So they tell me."

"Sister Jeanette found her this morning?"

"Right."

"Where's Jeanette?"

"At St. Ad's."

"I've got to get out there. Are you going to stick around for the funeral, Frances?''

"Yes."

"You want to stay at my house? They'll probably have a house full at St. Ad's. Alumnae. Nuns. Ex-nuns. Relatives. Do you have any out-of-town relatives, Jack?''

"A few. I guess I should get on the phone and call them."

"What about it, Frances?"

"I think I'll stay in the dorm. Thank you, anyway. I'm settled in, and Zita might need my help with making beds or something."

"I'd love to have you, if you change your mind."

"Thank you."

"Do you think that scene last night got Mother Celeste so worked up that she jumped off the porch? Committed suicide like Barb?''

I was surprised to hear Pauline talk about it so casually in front of Jack. I said, "I don't know. I left right after the meeting."

"With Jack. I heard. I heard about you two slow dancing at the club last night."

"Did you talk to Mother Celeste after the meeting?" I asked.

"Yes. I was so furious. I could have killed her. Sorry, Jack. I didn't mean that. That's a terrible thing to say. Did Frances tell you about the meeting?"

"I saw your car there. And the Rolls. And Tom's heap."

"Well, you probably know about my sister anyway. I know you're discreet. Barbara killed herself. I've suspected all along. Now it turns out she left notes for all of us, and Sharon kept the notes. I don't blame her. Not really. I know my parents put pressure on the nuns to let people think Barbara died a natural death. Mother Celeste drove my sister to suicide. It's as simple as that. I've got to go. I've got to get busy." She turned and left.

We watched her drive down the street in the direction of St. Adelaide's. After a few minutes, we saw Eddie Braddock pull out of the funeral home parking lot and turn towards the square.

In the kitchen, the doughnut bag and the coffee cup were on the table. Eddie had left a mess for his nephews to clean up.

Jack said, "Do you think Pauline killed my aunt?"

"Possibly."

"We should find out what the notes said. The person who got the worst note was probably the one who killed Mother Celeste."

"You could be right. I want to take a look at the

place where they found Mother Celeste's body. Then I'll get started asking questions. You're sure you want me to tell people you're my client?''

"Sure. That's the truth. Tell people I hired you to look into the circumstances surrounding my great-aunt's death. We won't say we think she was murdered. That would just get Randy Hermann involved and cause an autopsy. We don't want to delay the funeral. We want the funeral out of the way so Sister Sharon can get on with things. What about just saying someone was seen on the convent steps? Say I hired you to find out who that was. Say I want to talk to that person to see if he saw Mother Celeste outside her door. Say I want to be reassured that Mother Celeste didn't suffer. I don't care what you say. Say the truth. Say I think my great-aunt was murdered. If people are already talking about it in the doughnut shack, it won't seem the least bit strange that I'm interested in finding out what really happened. How could an old woman who could barely walk from her bed to a chair get across a big wide porch in the rain?''

"I hope it's not too much for Sharon.''

"Me too. I can't figure out why Mother Celeste would try to pin the blame on Sharon for Barbara Ross's death. It was like she was trying to kill Sharon with stress. It sounds to me like Mother Celeste got what was coming to her.''

"That's the way I feel, too. I'm sorry, Jack.''

He finished loading the dishwasher. He put in soap and closed it. He cleaned the sink and the counter. "Don't apologize. The Braddocks don't age well. My grandmother, Mother Celeste's sister, was a mean old bitch in old age. She pulled a trick or two with her will. And my grandpa and my dad didn't age well, either.

The Braddocks don't age well. I'd like to get this straightened out for Sister Sharon's sake. She was good to me when I was in first grade. She'd stop by here on her way to school. We'd walk to school together. Usually Pauline would walk with us. Pauline and I would stand out on our porches in the morning, waiting for Sharon to come from St. Ad's. She and the other nun who taught at St. George's would walk with us to school. Sharon would hold my hand. She'd talk to me about my mother when no one else would. I know you know about that. Losing your mother when you're little sets you apart. People are afraid to mention it. Like if they mentioned it, I'd be reminded of her. As if I wasn't thinking about her all the time. I wanted to talk about her. Sharon was the only one who would. I don't like it that Mother Celeste decided to try to get her in trouble. Acted out her own problems on Sharon. Blamed her for something she didn't do. Couldn't do. There are a lot of things about this whole deal I don't like. Did you say there was no letter for Mother Celeste?"

"I did."

"What do you figure that means?"

"Maybe that Barbara had already told Mother Celeste she was going to kill herself. In person. No need for a note."

"I'll help you investigate. Don't worry about money. I think I told you I made a little money on the interstate. Let's get started."

I went out to the car to get a contract.

When I got back inside, Zita and Al were in the kitchen with Jack. Mother Celeste's body was ready to be returned to St. Adelaide's. Al had called the convent. The nuns would be in the chapel at noon to receive the body.

Jack explained to his brother that he was hiring me to question people who had spoken to Mother Celeste in the hours before her death. He told him about the person Zita and I had seen on the steps. Al agreed that the matter should be investigated. He suggested that I be hired by both brothers. I agreed to that, and we signed a contract.

At ten minutes to twelve, Jack and Al put the coffin containing Mother Celeste's body in the hearse. The coffin was not cardboard, but dark wood. Sister Zita rode in the hearse with Jack and Al. I followed in my car.

Jack and Al removed the coffin from the hearse and wheeled it along the ground floor corridor to the elevator. I followed with the nuns who had been waiting at the south door. There was not enough room in the elevator for everyone, so Zita and I went up the steps to the first-floor rotunda. The chapel doors were open, and we went in. Sister Sharon and the other nuns were waiting.

After a minute of two, Jack and Al wheeled the coffin up the center aisle to the catafalque. The chaplain stood there with an aspergillum in his hand. Jack and Al lifted the coffin off the rolling cart and placed it on the catafalque. The sacristan moved the tall, wooden candlesticks into place around the coffin. She lit the dark beeswax candles and stepped back. Al Braddock opened the top section of the coffin. The chaplain blessed the corpse and sprinkled it with holy water.

Sister Sharon and the other councilors went up to look at the body. The other nuns followed. There were a few other people in the chapel, men and women from the town. They went up to look at the corpse, and I went along.

Mother Celeste was dressed in the habit the Ade-laides wore until the late sixties. The scroll of parch-ment on which she had written her vows seventy-five years earlier was in her hands. Al had done a good job with her face. She looked like she did in the parlor the first time I met her.

When all the nuns and visitors were back in their pews, Sharon intoned the midday prayer from the office of the dead. The nuns took up the chant. Jack and Al knelt in the front pew throughout the brief prayer, and when the nuns left the chapel to go down to the refec-tory, they followed.

Sharon invited them to stay for Sunday dinner, and they accepted.

I needed to be alone. I told Sharon I had to go home to get some clothes and check on my mail.

FIFTEEN

I DROVE HOME on the old highway. I drove slowly, forty miles an hour. I had my little tape recorder on, and I talked as I drove, listing suspects in the murder of Mother Celeste. I recorded the questions I intended to ask them.

By the time I reached Metcalf, I was recording myself singing. I switched off the recorder. Why was I so happy? Someone had died. Or been murdered. Had Mother Celeste been murdered? Did I care? I felt nothing for Mother Celeste other than resentment left over from boarding school days and anger over her attempt to use me to hurt Sharon. Even the anger was not intense. People over ninety get a pass.

I was happy because I had an excuse to stick around Braddock for three more days. I had decided to spend no more than three days on the case. My usual time schedule with adoption searches was a week. Most people could afford me for a week. Sometimes I found what they were looking for in a day. If a week went by without results, I knew I would be unlikely to find their answers. In this case, the number of suspects was limited, and they all lived within a few blocks of one another. I could see them all in one day. If I hadn't learned anything in three days, I probably wouldn't. The possibility existed that the person on the motherhouse steps *had* been a bum. He could have tossed Mother Celeste over the railing or watched her jump or watched her have a heart attack and then fall over. That person could be in Kansas City or Tulsa or God knows where by now. I would never find out anything. Three days would have to do it.

I was happy because I felt like I was on vacation. Even though I would be investigating a suspicious death, I would be on vacation. It would be a change from my real world of children abandoned long ago still wondering why.

Did the murderous instincts of a dysfunctional family frighten me? The situation was too unreal to take seriously. At St. Adelaide's, I was a pampered girl again, Zita's pet. I was a senior at the academy, slipping off on Sunday afternoons to walk on country roads with a boy from the local high school. It was nice to have Jack Braddock's interest again. And it was exciting to be a bit player in a big production, the funeral of a religious superior. It was nice to be on a case where my client was an attractive man. It was exciting to be investigating a murder, particularly one in which no one was too upset about the victim's death.

I would stay until Mother Celeste was buried. I didn't expect to discover anything conclusive. No one would break down under my questioning and admit to murder. I would probably not bring a killer to justice, but I would do my best to learn the identity of the person on the convent steps. If I came up with anything, I would present my client with my information, and let him decide what to do with it.

I knew Jack Braddock liked the idea of having me around for a few more days. His sweet and easy life could use a little excitement. Just a little. Three days worth.

I had nothing going on in Kansas City. I drove along the endless strip mall called Metcalf. I remembered how it looked when it was a highway, and horses grazed behind white fences. I remembered how caramel corn men once sold their confection along the road on summer Sundays like this one. I remembered how my parents would stop to buy the caramel corn for their little girl in the back seat.

I turned right at Seventy-fifth and left at Ward Parkway. I reached the Plaza and turned up Wornall. I parked in front of my house. There was mail all over the front hall.

I made a few phone calls. I read the mail. I watered the plants. I took a shower and packed. What to wear to a summer funeral? What to wear to investigate a murder? At the last minute, I thought about something my dad had told me once. I went back upstairs for my Smith and Wesson Thirty-eight.

I headed back to Braddock. It was five-thirty when I got there. I drove to St. George's and sat in my car watching the people who had attended the five o'clock mass come out of the little church.

Tom Ross, dressed in a green chasuble, stood on the sidewalk shaking hands with his parishioners. He went back inside the church when everyone had gone. After a few minutes, I went in. He was in the sacristy. "Ms. Finn," he said. His face was flushed. His gray eyes were bloodshot.

"Father Ross. Good afternoon."

"What can I do for you?" He took off his wrinkled alb and laid it on top of the chasuble on the vestment case.

"I wonder if I could ask you a question."

"Certainly. Would you care to join me for dinner? I'm about to barbecue a couple of prime lamb chops."

I didn't want to eat with this man who had behaved

so badly the day before, but how else was I going to get a look at his sister's suicide note? "Thank you, Father. I'd like that very much."

"Please call me Tom. Everybody does."

We left the church and walked across the mowed lawn to the rectory.

The house was freezing inside. Like many men who live alone, Tom Ross overdid the air-conditioning. And like many priests, he overdid the interior decoration. He shared his parents' taste for things Victorian, but the cold little ranch house was not the setting for chintz slipcovers and lace curtains.

We went through the house to the backyard. The fire was ready. He had lit it before he went over to say mass. Potatoes wrapped in foil were roasting in the coals. Had he planned to eat two? Now he placed four mammoth lamb chops on the grill.

The food smelled wonderful, and I found that I was very hungry. I had skipped lunch. Tom Ross mixed a gin and tonic for me. He was drinking Scotch on the rocks. He brought out a salad and tossed it with dressing he had made. He turned the lamb chops and put plates and cutlery on the picnic table.

While we ate, Tom Ross told me about his plans for the funeral. The rabid tone of the night before was gone. Now he was excited, the busy host. "I've got four priests coming in tomorrow, and two more on Tuesday. Just about every priest in Kansas and Missouri will be here. A few from Oklahoma. A guy from San Antone. I've been on the phone all day. The bishop and his bunch will stay at St. Ad's, of course, and the order men will stay at the chaplain's, but I'll have a good group out here. Nothing like a big funeral to liven things up. No pun intended."

What pun? Where's the letter?

"Dessert should be here any minute," he said, looking at his watch. "One of the women is bringing over a strawberry pie. And homemade ice cream to go with it."

Perfect timing. The life of a small town priest is filled with food. No wonder this peculiar man was so enormous. A woman drove up in a pickup truck just as Tom Ross was bringing out the coffee. She put the pie and ice cream on the table. She declined to join us. "I've got to get my own supper on the table, Father," she said.

After she drove off, Tom Ross went back inside and came out with a bottle of brandy and two snifters.

I sat there eating and drinking with him, deciding he wasn't a murderer after all. Maybe he was just another lonely priest. Stuck down here in Braddock, Kansas, he had nothing to do but eat and drink and mow the lawn and brood about his dead twin. I moved him down from his top position on my list of suspects. He wasn't as smart as Pauline, or as cruel as Peter, or as dumb as Winnie. Which one of them had seen Mother Celeste last? After a few sips of brandy, I said, "Last night must have been very shocking for you."

"Isn't that what you intended?"

"Well, I didn't intend anything. I came down here because Mother Celeste wanted to talk to me. I didn't know about what."

"Now you know."

"I don't really."

"I told you half of me is dead." He had not eaten like a man half dead. "The only thing that has kept me going all these years was thinking Sharon Bieralski killed Barbara. Now, I don't even have that." Twenty

minutes earlier he had been bursting with excitement
over the expected house guests. Now, he was morose.

"How could you think Sharon could kill anyone?"

"You don't understand."

"What did your sister say in her note?" I might as
well come right out and ask. I didn't want to hear another diatribe about Sharon. Tom Ross was on his second large brandy, and his eyes were getting weirder
than ever.

"You think Sharon is so wonderful. Tell me this.
How could she keep my sister's farewell message from
me for thirty years? Let me think Barbara left me without a word of explanation. Keep me in the dark. Keep
me from knowing why half of me was dead."

"Did you go in to talk to Mother Celeste last night?"

"Of course."

"How did she seem?"

He didn't answer. He just stared into his brandy snifter.

SIXTEEN

THE SUN WAS going down. I could see that Tom Ross
was not going to say anything else. I hadn't mentioned
to him that I was investigating Mother Celeste's death.
I thought I might confer again with my clients before
mentioning my investigation to anyone. They might be
having second thoughts.

I thanked Tom Ross for dinner and left him sitting
alone in his yard with his brandy snifter.

I parked in front of the funeral home. Across the
street, Winnie Ross was sitting on her front porch. She
waved to me, and I crossed the street.

"Frances," she called.

I unlatched the gate and walked up to the porch. Winnie's son had been well lit when I left him, and she
seemed to be at about the same point. She was drinking
Scotch.

"Would you like a drink?"

"No, thank you." I sat down next to her on the
swing. It was nearly dark now, and I could see Jack
Braddock in the light of an upstairs window of the funeral home, sitting at a desk.

"You're staying for the funeral?"

"Yes."

Winnie Ross was perfectly groomed and wearing
high heels. She said, "I expect people will be coming
from all over. It's the end of an era."

"You spoke to Mother Celeste after the meeting last
night?"

"Yes. I was beside myself. As I'm sure you noticed."

I watched Jack Braddock. He stood up and turned off the light. In a minute, I saw the kitchen light go on. I said, "It must have been very shocking to read Sister Barbara's letter after all these years."

"Would you like to see it?"

"Yes."

She had it in her pocket. She handed it to me. I stood up to examine the letter in the light coming from the living room window. The envelope was addressed to Winifred A. Ross. Winnie had not torn the envelope open but had slit it neatly at the top. With what? I wondered.

Sister Barbara's last words to her mother were written on one side of a six by eight sheet of paper, folded once. The paper matched the envelope. It was the stationery used at St. Adelaide's, cream colored, with the order's coat of arms embossed at the top.

Sister Barbara had used black ink in her fountain pen.

November 30, 1965

Mama,

I wish you and Dad had taken me home this afternoon. I knew you wouldn't, but I thought I would try one last time to make you understand. After you left, Mother Celeste told me you and Dad agreed with her that I should go to St Michael's. I can't go there, Mama. I tried to make that clear to you. For me, life in that place would be worse than death. I can't pretend to be mentally ill. I am perfectly clear in my mind. I'm not afraid to die. Don't cry, Mama. We are together forever.

Barbara

Winnie's back was to me as I stood by the window. I read the note a few times. Then I folded it and put it back in the envelope. I handed it back to Winnie as I sat down.

She said, "If I could turn back the clock."

I said, "What is St. Michael's?"

"St. Michael's was a mental hospital in St. Louis that specialized in treating nuns and priests. I don't think it exists anymore. Barbara and some of the other nuns used to sing there at Sunday mass when they were in St. Louis at summer school. Barbara hated going there. She told me it was a real snake pit. She told me once about a nun she saw there who scratched her arms constantly. They were like raw meat."

"You knew Mother Celeste was going to put her there?"

"Mother Celeste told us Barbara needed psychiatric treatment. Mother Celeste had talked to a psychiatrist, and he said Barbara needed to be hospitalized." Winnie took another sip of Scotch.

Across the street, Jack Braddock opened the kitchen door and came down to the curb with bags of trash. He noticed my car and looked around. He saw me on the Rosses' porch. "Evening, Mrs. Ross. Frances."

"Come on over, Jack, and have a drink," Winnie said.

"Thanks." He opened the gate and came up to the porch.

"Are you sure you won't have anything, Frances?"

"I'm sure. Thanks."

Winnie went inside with her glass in her hand. Her high heels tapped on the wooden floor inside.

"Where have you been?" Jack asked. He sat on the porch railing.

"I drove up to Kansas City to get some clothes. When I got back, I dropped in on Tom Ross." I whispered. I wasn't sure I wanted Winnie or Peter to know I had talked to their son. Where was Peter? "What have you been doing?"

"Making some phone calls. I called the Braddocks, and Al called the Walshes. There aren't too many relatives left. We've got a couple of cousins that are going to come."

Winnie came outside with a tray. She had glasses, Cokes, and a bottle of rum. "I know you like Cuba Libres, Jack, and I thought Frances might have a plain Coke if she won't drink with us."

Jack took the tray from her and poured drinks. Winnie had turned off the light inside. It had been attracting June bugs. Now we sat in the dusk. The sound of the cicadas in the trees rose and fell. If I could turn back the clock. How far back? If I could turn it back a hundred years, this house would be here, looking just the same. The Braddocks' house across the street would be the same. The town square and the two hotels and the militiaman and the *Braddock Herald* would all be the same. The ancestors of the cicadas would be singing the same song. St. Ad's would not be there. The founders would not have left Kentucky. The campus would be a corn field.

The clock could not be turned back. I could see that the letter was still in Winnie's pocket. A nun had written a last, brief, cold note to her mother. Had Winnie killed Mother Celeste? Mother Celeste's threat to put Barbara Ross in a mental hospital had driven her to suicide. If I had a daughter, and someone drove her to commit suicide, I would kill that person with my bare hands.

I finished my drink. Winnie was telling Jack about a party she was planning for the bishop the night before the funeral. She invited us to attend. Finally I said, "I've got to go, Mrs. Ross. I'd like to talk to you again, if that would be okay."

"Please come by tomorrow, Frances. Peter goes to the *Herald* at about eleven. That would be a good time for us to talk."

Jack undraped himself from the railing. "I'll say good-night, too, Mrs. Ross. Thanks for the drink." He walked to the car with me. "I'll ride out to St. Ad's with you and walk back. Okay? I can use the exercise."

"Sure."

"Want me to drive?"

I handed him the keys. He pulled away from the curb slowly, driving my car as carefully as he drove the funeral cars. "This windshield is dirty."

"Bugs from the highway."

"Let's go by the station and gas her up and wipe the windshield. Okay?"

"Sure."

The gas station was open. A boy was sitting at the desk reading a magazine. He got up to take care of my car, and Jack took the money out of the cash drawer. "Have you eaten?"

"With Tom Ross. He grilled lamb chops."

"Did you ask him what his letter said?"

"He wouldn't tell me. I didn't feel like really quizzing him until I talked to you again."

"About what?"

"Well, I wanted to be sure you still want me to investigate."

The boy came inside. I paid for the gas, and Jack and

I went back to the car. He drove down the old highway a few miles. "Mind if I open her up a little?"

"Be my guest." My car had never had such an opportunity to display its abilities before.

Jack said, "We want to go ahead with it. We talked about it again this afternoon. I explained the whole thing again to Al. He said he doesn't think Mother Celeste would have gotten so broken up if she had just had a heart attack and fallen off the porch. It's more like someone threw her down. Tried to hurt her. Al wants to go ahead and so do I. You can tell Sharon as much or as little as you think she can take. You're the pro."

"I'll have to tell people I question that I'm working for you. Will that hurt you?"

"Businesswise?"

"Or socially."

"I'm a social zero as it is. And a business minus sign. The gas station doesn't make any money. As far as the funeral home goes, it's the only one in town. Sooner or later, everyone dies, and the Braddock brothers get 'em. Go ahead and tell people you're working for me. I don't care what they think. The only one who's going to mind is the murderer."

"I've got to get back. I want to talk to Sister Zita tonight."

Jack turned the car around, and drove back to the convent. As we pulled up in front of the old convent, Jack said, "Does a client get a good-night kiss, or would that be unprofessional?"

I kissed him on the cheek. He was as fragrant as he had been in high school. We got out of the car and walked up to the porch. Sister Zita was sitting on the glider. I sat on the steps, and Jack sat on the railing.

"So?" I asked Zita. "How was your afternoon?"

"Long. I just thought I'd sit out here and rest my bones and wait for you. Have you eaten? I've got some peanut butter inside."

"I'm not hungry. Thanks."

"Jack?"

"Peanut butter sounds good to me, Sister."

"I've got some lunch meat over at Father's. Would that be better? I could make us some sandwiches."

"I've got a better idea," Jack said. "What about all three of us going to the A and W? I could go for a Papa Burger."

Zita was on her feet. I didn't feel like going out again, but I couldn't deny her the pleasure of a grease feast.

While we waited for the car hop to bring our food, Zita told us about the afternoon and evening. People from the town had been visiting the chapel to view the body and sign the book. Peter Ross had knelt in the chapel for an hour and then had gone to the graveyard. He sat on a bench down there for another hour.

Zita had spent the afternoon making up beds in the old convent and in the chaplain's house. Visitors would begin arriving Monday morning.

Sharon had spent the afternoon in bed. Zita had run into Sister Jeanette in the linen room and had heard from her that Sharon was blaming herself for Mother Celeste's supposed heart attack.

I drank root beer while Jack and Zita ate Papa Burgers. After I dropped Jack off at the funeral home, I asked Zita if the feet she saw could have been wearing high heels. She didn't think so.

I parked in front of the old convent. I took my suitcase and my garment bag out of the trunk and carried them up to the door. Zita opened the door for me and then went into the infirmary. I went up the steps to the third floor.

SEVENTEEN

SOMEONE HAD BEEN in my room. Not Zita. She would have replaced the asters with fresh ones. She would have turned down the bed. Someone else had been in the room. I sensed it immediately.

I opened the door to the wardrobe. The person who had been in my room had opened the door. I could tell because it was closed more securely than I ever closed it. I had avoided closing this door tightly since the first day of sophomore year. Two pieces of hardware closing together made a rasping sound that I couldn't stand. When I had packed my bag earlier in the day, I had left only my suit hanging in the wardrobe. It was hanging now at a slightly different angle than it had earlier.

The dresser drawers were empty. I had taken the pajamas and underwear home that had been in the top drawer. I hadn't used the other drawers. I opened them now. They were lined with tissue paper. I couldn't tell if anyone had looked in those drawers. I opened the little drawer in the desk. That drawer was lined with a piece of green blotting paper cut about an inch smaller than the drawer. I could see that it had been moved. Someone had looked under it and replaced it closer to one side than it had been before.

The book I had been reading, *Tom Playfair*, was on the nightstand still, but closer to the edge than it had been before. There was nothing else in the room.

I started trembling. The realization that I might be in

danger grabbed me and shook me free of the stupid illusion of being on vacation.

I put my suitcase and garment bag on the bed. I kept my purse on my arm. The weight of the Smith and Wesson reassured me somewhat. I examined the screen on the window. It was locked. The person who had been in my room had left by the door to the hall, not by the window to the fire escape.

I went out into the hall. The dim light overhead was not enough to banish the shadows. I opened each door and turned on the lights in each room. Zita had not made up the beds in these rooms. On each one was a bare mattress.

I checked the bathroom. There were innumerable hiding places in this antique building. There was the attic, for one thing. I remembered sneaking up there to smoke on days too cold for the fire escape. There were rows of glass-fronted bookcases up there filled with school books from the days when St. Ad's had grammar school children as well as high school girls. There were big tables where novices had ironed and folded sheets long ago. There were cabinets where linens had been stored.

On this floor, in addition to the boarders' rooms at this end, there were classrooms and the library at the other end. The chapel-turned-library was two stories high. You could enter from the second floor or from this floor. The third-floor door opened into the former choir loft. In my school days, bound volumes of magazines were kept there.

On the second floor, there were boarders' rooms, doubles. Four girls had lived in each of those rooms. There were classrooms down there as well, and the main floor of the library. The library had offices behind it in the rooms that once had been the sacristies.

On the first floor of the old convent were more offices, the big parlor, small parlors, classrooms, and the infirmary. There were staircases at either end of the building with closets underneath. There were bathrooms, storage rooms, an ancient elevator, and the passageway to the auditorium building. The auditorium building was another warren of possible hiding places for murderers. There were dorms, music rooms, a stage with dressing rooms backstage, and below, a gym with locker rooms.

On the ground floor of the old convent were the boiler room, the art room, the little store, a little kitchen for the boarders, the costume room where dozens of murderers could hide and disguise themselves, and the entrance to the tunnel.

I stood shaking in the hall. I heard Zita coming up the stairs.

She came down the hall, saw all the doors open and all the lights on. "What's wrong?"

"Someone was in my room."

She didn't say, how can you tell? or anything like that. She said, "Well, we'll sleep in the motherhouse tonight."

"We will?"

"Follow me." We turned off the lights. I got my bags. We went down to the infirmary. Zita said, "I didn't make the beds up there. I figured the ones I made on the second floor would be enough. We won't have more than ten or fifteen people in this building."

"Who was over here?"

"I didn't see anyone. But I was in and out all day, all over the place. Someone could easily have been up there, and I wouldn't see them. There were people around all day, strangers, in and out of the chapel all day. Anybody could have come over here through the tunnel. Did they take anything?"

"There wasn't anything to take. I took my laundry home. But I think what they were looking for was a piece of paper."

"What makes you think that?"

"Because they looked under the blotter in the desk drawer. Nothing would fit under there but a piece of paper."

Zita got her robe and pajamas. She went into her bathroom for her toiletries. She got towels and wash-cloths from a drawer. She said, "Sometimes in the winter I get too cold over here. They don't fire up the boiler anymore. I have a space heater in here, but if it gets too cold for that, I go over and sleep in the novitiate. It's empty. We'll be safe over there."

She locked the door to the infirmary. She checked the front door to make sure it was locked. We went downstairs and through the tunnel. As we walked along the ground floor of the motherhouse, I said, "Did you ever look in Sister Barbara's trunk?"

"No. Do you want to?"

"Would it be all right?"

"Who's going to know?" The four corridors of the X-shaped building came together at the rotunda. The ground floor rotunda had doors to the refectory on one side and doors to the trunk room on the other. The refectory was under the chapel, and the trunk room was under the front porch.

Zita pulled a string to turn on the light. The long, narrow room had trunks and suitcases lined up in rows. Big doors in the fourth wall opened to meat lockers where sides of beef had been refrigerated in the old days. A history of luggage could be written in that room. The wooden trunks at the far end of the room had domed tops and leather straps. The leather trunks in the middle rows had flat tops and decorative brass hardware. The most recent trunks were plain, made of black metal with aluminum bands. Zita went to a trunk in the middle range. "This is mine," she said. "Sister Barbara's should be one of these." She looked at the tags on a few trunks. "Here it is." She opened the lid. It wasn't locked.

We looked in Sister Barbara's trunk. There were a few folded tee-shirts and black petticoats in the trunk, two flannel nightgowns, some books, and several note-books, spiral and looseleaf. I opened a notebook. "Her college notes," I said. Another folder held lesson-plan books.

"Not much."

"They probably looked in it when she died," Zita said. "This is just stuff they never got around to getting rid of."

"Can I take these notebooks upstairs?"

"Help yourself."

Zita closed the trunk. I went over to the little window, and looked out. The porch light was on, so I could see the stone steps outside the window. Zita turned off the light in the trunk room. "See how I could see?" she asked.

I could. While we were watching, a man and woman went down the steps. It was possible to see their legs up to knee level. "Where were you standing?" I asked.

"Here." Under the light string. It was possible to see two steps from there.

We took the elevator up to the third floor. I had never been above the first floor of the motherhouse before. I looked over the railing in the rotunda. There was a rail-

ing exactly the same on the floor below, and below that
was the first-floor rotunda, the area between the front
door and the chapel. There were a few people standing
there. I could hear them talking softly. One of them was
Eddie Braddock.

"What's he doing?" I whispered to Zita.

"He's been here all day," she said. "Greeting people
who come to look at Mother."

She led me down a hall exactly like the infirmary hall
downstairs. Door after door, each opened to a small
single room. "I always sleep here," she said at the door
to the last room in the hall. "Two windows. Cross ven-
tilation. Why don't you take the room across from
mine?" She opened the door to another corner room
with a single bed, a dresser, a little desk, and a straight
chair.

I put my bag on the floor. Zita hung my garment bag
in the closet. She turned back the cover of the bed to
make sure it was made. I put the notebooks on the desk.

Zita said, "No one will come up here. The nuns coming from Kansas City and St. Louis will sleep on the
second floor. It's too hot up here for them. You don't
mind, do you? I'll show you the bathroom."

She gave me towels and washcloths. "You got sham-
poo and toothpaste?"

"Everything I need. Thank you." Suddenly I felt like
I had to lie down.

"Give yourself a good rest," Zita said. "No one will
find us up here." She went into her room and closed
the door.

I went into my room. I looked out the window. This
room was two floors above the convent infirmary. It was
in the same position as the room Sister Barbara and
Mother Celeste had occupied. I opened the windows.

People were getting in their cars and driving away. The last one to go was Eddie Braddock.

I unpacked my bags. I took a shower in the novices' bathroom. When I was in school, my friends and I spent a good deal of time wondering about the novices' lives. There were novices and postulants in some of our classes. Some were former classmates, no longer allowed to talk to us. They sat in class with us and participated in class discussions, but after class they returned to the mysterious realm of the novitiate. Now here I was. The novices and postulants had better showers than the boarders and nicer rooms. But there were no more novices or postulants at St. Adelaide's and no more boarding school girls.

I went back to my room, closed the door, and moved the dresser against the door. I loaded my gun and placed it on the desk next to my bed. I turned off the ceiling light and lit the gooseneck lamp on the desk. I got into bed and started looking through Barbara Ross's notebooks.

Her college notes were careful and detailed. She had majored in English at an all-nuns' college in St. Louis. I couldn't tell if she had completed a degree or not. There was a copy of the school literary magazine for summer 1960. It had poetry, book reviews, and essays by nuns of various orders. There was a poem about fishing by Sister M. Barbara Ross, R.S.A.

There were grade books and lesson-plan books from St. George's. Sister Barbara taught grades one through four in the two-room school. There was a folder of notes from the novitiate, and a notebook full of mimeographed pages of convent regulations about housecleaning, food service, travel, home visits, every detail of life.

I could see that a person who liked making decisions for herself would find it hard living in an institution that had a rule about how to raise and lower venetian blinds.

EIGHTEEN

IN THE MORNING, I put my gun back in my purse. I moved the dresser away from the door. I went to the window and looked down. The sun was shining, and a man was riding a huge lawn mower around the campus. I looked down at the porch. I could see the top of St. Adelaide's head. I had never seen it before. The academy girls always painted her crown gold for her feast-day, December sixteenth, but I had never been the one chosen to go up the ladder to do it. Her hair, which she wore in long braids, was parted in the center.

I took a shower, and got dressed. The house phone buzzed outside my door. I answered it.

It was Zita. "Come over to Father's when you're ready," she said. "I'll fry you some scrapple."

I stopped by my car to phone for messages. In the little kitchen of the chaplain's residence, I ate waffles and scrapple and read Mother Celeste's obituary in the *Kansas City Journal-Post*.

Mother Mary Celeste Walsh, superior of St. Adelaide's Convent in Braddock, Kansas, died Sunday at the motherhouse following a long illness.

Mother Walsh was born in Braddock in 1897, and attended St. Adelaide's Academy from her early childhood until her graduation in 1913. She entered the Sisters of St. Adelaide in 1914, and made vows in 1917.

Mother Walsh received a bachelor's degree from

the old St. Genevieve's College in Kansas City, and a master's degree and doctorate from Catholic University in Washington, D.C. She was the recipient of several honorary degrees as well.

Mother Walsh taught English at St. Adelaide's Academy from 1920 until the boarding school closed in 1977. She was the author of *Walsh's Creek*, a best-selling novel of 1950, and *Decades of Joy*, a history of the Sisters of St. Adelaide in America. In addition to her books, Mother Walsh wrote many articles on Kansas history.

Mother Walsh was elected superior of her congregation in 1933, and remained in office until her death. She is survived by nephews and cousins.

There will be visitation in the convent chapel at Braddock on Monday and Tuesday. There will be a funeral mass on Wednesday at 10:00 a.m. Burial will follow in the convent cemetery.

Zita was cleaning the waffle iron. Her back was to me.

"Several honorary degrees," I said.

Zita snorted.

"Can I ask you a personal question?" I had never asked Zita about her life, but I was curious about one thing in particular.

"What is it?"

"Why didn't you go to school?" All the Adelaides went to school. They piled up degree upon degree. The nuns went to summer school throughout their lives. Every May, the academy girls would hear from their teachers about their plans for summer school. They all went to school. Everyone but the kitchen sisters and Zita.

She didn't turn around. She finished cleaning the waffle iron and then started on the coffee maker. Finally she said, "I had a dowry."

"What does that mean?"

"Just like the sisters who entered right out of high school. But I was thirty-two when I entered. Mother Celeste had the idea that since I had been a servant in a doctor's house, I should be a servant in the convent. She even picked a servant's name for me: Zita. Saint Zita is the patron saint of servants. Most Adelaides keep their own names in religious life, but Mother Celeste decided to call me Zita. My name is Elizabeth. Even though I had a dowry just like girls who entered right out of high school, Mother Celeste never let me go to school. When the other second-year novices would be taking classes—they used to take extension courses in the novitiate in those days, I would have to go downstairs to help Jeanette in the infirmary or go outside and take care of the horses. When my classmates were sent out to teach, I was put in charge of the laundry. I had a dowry, but Mother Celeste never let me go to school."

"God, what a waste," I said. Zita was smart.

She wiped her eyes on her apron. She turned to face me. The shame on her face made me want to cry, too. Why hadn't she complained? Why hadn't she insisted on an education? I knew the answer. The superior took the place of God. The vow of obedience meant do what you were told.

I said, "Mother Celeste was mean." I wanted to get up and hug Zita, but our relationship was not like that. I was not a natural hugger, and she was not a natural huggee.

"She thought because she was a Braddock, she was better than anyone else." Zita's voice was always ironic, but now there was a bitterness I had not heard before.

Did Zita kill Mother Celeste? She could have gone over to the motherhouse Saturday night, through the tunnel, up to Mother Celeste's room. She could have opened the door to the porch if it was closed, picked up Mother Celeste from her bed, dropped her over the railing, and then started down the steps. Zita was little, but she was strong. She used to milk the cows, push the horses into their stalls, force the pigs back from the fence when she threw in their food. When she saw Jack's car, she could have run back up the steps, back through Mother Celeste's room, and back over to the old convent through the tunnel. She could have told me about seeing someone from the trunk room window to cover herself.

Would I blame her for seeking revenge? She had been made to spend her life in the barnyard instead of in the classroom. She had entered the convent with a dowry like a choir nun, but she had been treated like a lay sister. Mother Celeste had refused her the opportunity to get an education and become a teacher in an order of teachers.

Zita had taken care of me when I was a motherless girl at boarding school. She had helped me through adolescence. She had given me tea and peanut butter. She had told me the facts of life.

Mother Celeste had disliked me and criticized me. The assignments I wrote for her English class were never good enough. The articles and editorials I wrote for the *Crown* were never good enough. When I was about to graduate from the academy, I asked her to write a letter of recommendation to the college I planned to go to. She wrote a bad letter. She told them I never worked up to my ability. When the president of the college showed me the letter a couple of years later, she said, "I think you should know about this so you never make the mistake of asking this Mother Celeste to recommend you for anything again."

Mother Celeste's dislike for me survived the years. When she was at death's door, she selected me to be her instrument for attacking someone else she disliked: Sharon. Would I blame Zita if she had killed Mother Celeste? I would not. But I didn't think Zita was capable of murder.

She said, "Are you going to tell Sister Sharon you're investigating?"

"I've got to. I'm going to question the Rosses today, and I'll have to tell them what I'm doing. I've got to tell Sharon before somebody else does."

"I'll walk over with you. I've got to take a look at the bishop's department." Back to work.

We walked across the lilac field and around by the barnyard. The brown hens squawked in alarm as we passed. The parking lot was already full of cars. We went in the south door and up the stairs to the first floor. At the end of the northwest corridor was a suite of rooms reserved for the bishop.

"Wow." I had never seen this before, either. The furniture was high Victorian, elaborately carved, upholstered with red plush. Heavy lace curtains hung on the windows. Each chair had an embroidered and tasseled antimacassar. There were little footstools covered with needlepoint.

"Pretty fancy, isn't it?" Zita opened the windows to air the rooms. While she checked the bedroom and bathroom, I studied the past bishops whose oval-framed pictures decorated the sitting room. The first bishop, the one who had permitted the founders to establish the Adelaides in his diocese, had long blond ringlets like General Custer.

"I'm going to find Sharon," I said.

"She's probably in the office," Zita said.

I went down the hall to the rotunda. Eddie Braddock was there standing by the visitors' book. He was talking to some women who had come to view the body. He nodded to me as I passed.

Sharon was in the office on the phone. Several nuns were in there. Sharon hung up the phone and said to me, "Meet me outside by the statue. I'll be outside in five minutes."

I went back to the rotunda. Eddie Braddock was alone, paging through the book. He said, "A hundred signatures already. More than a hundred. I'm going to have to get another book. Most people are taking up four or five lines. They're writing little sentiments about my aunt."

"Well, she was a popular person," I said.

"Popular is the understatement of the year. I didn't think to save the first page for the bishop. I think I'll run uptown while there's a lull and get another book. I'll reserve the first few pages for the bishop and the clergy." He turned and left.

I read a few of the entries. "Her glorious smile welcomed me to the academy in 1938." "I'll never forget golden days under Mother's gentle care." "Farewell, sweet Mother Celeste, now in the Celestial Realm." Should I write in the book: "Good, but not your best"? No. I went outside.

I walked over to the statue, and looked at the place behind it where Mother Celeste's body had lain. There was no mark on the pavement. Then, something made me turn and look at the statue. On one of the back corners of the base, held fast by an irregularity in the stone, was a white hair.

NINETEEN

SHARON CAME outside. She walked quickly towards me. She took my hands and patted them. Sharon was a hugger and a patter.

"Are you feeling better?" I asked.

"I'm fine. I'm kind of excited. It's exciting having so many people around. This place has been so dead so long. It's terrible to say that, isn't it?"

"I have to show you something."

"What?"

"First, I should tell you something. Jack and Al Braddock have hired me to investigate the circumstances surrounding Mother Celeste's death."

"What circumstances?"

"Well, for one thing, they find it hard to believe Mother Celeste could have fallen over that high railing. Or even gotten to it, from her bed. She was so weak. How could she walk so far?"

"I've wondered the same thing."

"And how did she get that big gash on her head?"

"Hitting the ground, the doctor said."

"Look." I showed Sharon the white hair.

She understood the implication immediately. "Mother hit her head on the base of the statue."

"Right. But how did she get her head this far away from the wall if she fell over? She would have fallen straight down, not six feet out."

"What do you mean?"

"Mother's body was pretty broken up. Al and Jack

and Zita and I think someone pushed—I'd say threw—Mother Celeste off the porch. Threw her against the base of the statue. She hit her head on this corner and then hit the ground.''

Sharon was clutching my arms and staring into my face. ''Zita thinks that?''

''Zita and I both saw someone on the front steps Saturday night. Sunday morning. One o'clock. Probably the person who killed Mother Celeste.''

''Who was it?'' Sharon's soft brown eyes were filling with tears.

''We don't know. Zita was down there. In the trunk room.'' I pointed to the little basement window. ''She saw someone going down the steps. Lightning flashed, and she saw someone. I saw someone at the same instant. Jack and I had just driven in the back gate, and I was looking over in this direction. The lightning lit up a person on the steps.''

''It couldn't have been Mother.''

''No. It wasn't Mother. Whoever it was was in the middle of the steps. Even if Mother could have walked across the porch, and somehow down the steps, she would have been at the side. Holding onto the banister. I'd say she was already down here on the ground. The person, whoever it was, had already thrown her down.''

''Who was it?''

''That's what I'm going to find out. That's what Jack and Al have hired me to do. I wanted to clear it with you.''

She was staggering. I led her to the bench. ''Should we call the police?''

''That's up to you. There's no proof of anything. The hair is the only thing. Sister Jeanette said the force of the heart attack 'pitched' Mother off the porch. Whether a heart attack can pitch someone at an arc like that is something I couldn't say."

"No. It wouldn't." Sharon said. "You don't go flying through the air when you have a heart attack. You get totally weak. Everything fails. You collapse. Straight down."

"If we tell the police, they'll stop the funeral. Require an autopsy. If I were advising someone I didn't know or care about, I'd say tell the police. That would be to protect myself. But in this case, I'm suggesting we go ahead with the funeral. Say nothing. Meanwhile, I'll be asking questions in such a way that Randy Hermann won't feel threatened even if he hears about it. Who was on the steps? One simple question I'll be asking. If it was a bum, nobody will ever find him. Not the Braddock police. Certainly not me. If it was Peter Ross, we'll see."

"Peter Ross?"

"I'm going to talk to Winnie at eleven. Then Peter."

"You suspect them?"

"Of course. Think about it. Who else was so mad at Mother Celeste as the Rosses?"

"Winnie could never lift Mother and throw her over the railing like that."

"That's why we won't bother the police. What if we called Randy Hermann and said we think Winnie Ross did it? The idea of a tiny little woman in her seventies tossing another even tinier little woman in her nineties off a porch in the middle of a torrential downpour is not going to appeal to Chief Hermann. Especially when the tiny little murderer is the wife of the richest man in town."

"You think it was Winnie?"

"I can only go by experience. Revenge is powerful.

The need for revenge lasts through the years. It doesn't go away. Revenge is a dish best eaten cold. If you had a daughter, and someone drove her to suicide, wouldn't you kill that person?''

"Probably."

"I deal with mothers and daughters every day. Still brokenhearted about things that happened thirty, forty, fifty, seventy years ago. Still remember every detail. The way they were blindfolded when giving birth so they wouldn't know the sex of the baby. The way their babies sent mental telepathy to them after they gave them up for adoption. Come back. Come back. They'd still like to get revenge on the doctors and nurses and social workers who did those insane things to them all those years ago. And that's just over adoption. What about murder?''

"Being emotional gives you strength," Sharon said.

"That's right. Mothers lift cars off their kids that have been run over. I'd say it was Winnie. She's first on my list."

"Randy Hermann would think we were insane if we told him all this."

"We could never explain the whole thing to him."

"He isn't even Catholic."

We sat there rationalizing why we were going to go ahead with the funeral as planned. A group of women walked past and greeted Sharon. They were on their way inside to pay their respects.

When they were out of earshot, Sharon asked, "How do you know Mother Celeste drove Barbara to suicide?''

"I dropped in on Winnie last night. She showed me Barbara's note."

"What did it say?"

"Very short. Curt. Barbara said she'd rather be dead than go to St. Michael's. Did Mother Celeste really think Barbara was mentally ill?"

"Mother had a thing about psychiatry in those days. She made us all take tests. She was involved in the sister formation movement, and personality testing was a big part of that. The late fifties. Early sixties. That's when Mother built the juniorate in St. Louis. A place for the young nuns to live and go to school. She made us all take psychological tests. The Minnesota Multiphasic Personality Inventory. It had questions like, 'I think someone is following me: Some of the time. Most of the time. All of the time.' Mother made several nuns go see psychiatrists. Nearly as many were going to psychiatrists then as were going to chiropractors. She tried to get me to go to one once. No way was I going to spill my guts to some stranger who thinks women suffer from penis envy. Then have him run back to Mother Celeste and tell her what I said. That was one of the many times Mother Celeste was furious at me. I told her I thought psychology was on a par with phrenology."

"Barbara didn't want to go to a mental hospital?"

"She had nothing wrong with her mind."

"Why wouldn't her parents let her go home?"

"You don't know what it was like then. Leaving the convent was a disgrace. The vocation brochures said it wasn't, but it was. Ex-nuns were considered mentally disturbed. They were never allowed to come back to visit. They left by the back door when the rest of us were in chapel or something so no one would know when they left, or see them in secular clothes. We could never talk about a sister who left, never mention her name. It was like she never existed. It was so sick. Inhuman. And with Peter Ross, there was a real problem. He was afraid he'd lose his papal knighthood if she left. And if she left, Tommy would leave the priesthood. It was not to be considered. Peter told Barbara he would leave Winnie if she left the convent. He would disappear. They'd never see him again.''

"When did he tell her that?''

"Lots of times. When I was at their house the summer before Barbara made final vows, he told her that. It was terrible. The stability of the parents' marriage rested on Barbara staying in the convent. The whole week was a nightmare. I didn't stick around during the day. I'd come back out here during the day, but at night I'd have to go back uptown and sleep at the Rosses'. The screaming never stopped. Tommy was there, too. Well, you knew that, didn't you? Peter would be screaming. Winnie crying. Peter threatening. Barbara crying. Peter drinking. Tommy crying. Peter Ross is a monster.''

"Is he capable of murder?''

"I don't know. Then, I would have said *yes* without a second thought. Now, he's old. I can't be sure.''

Another car drove up the long drive, and parked in front. Two women went up the steps.

"So it's okay with you if I investigate?''

"Of course.'' She put her arm around me. "I'm so glad you're here. I'm sorry you got dragged into this whole thing, but I'm glad you're here. I guess it's selfish of me.''

"Why was Mother trying to hurt you?''

"She never liked me. It's a long story.''

"Please tell me.''

"I got off on the wrong foot with Mother Celeste from the start. When I first came to the academy, she wanted me to invite Eddie Braddock to a formal. I couldn't stand him. I told her I had already invited a cousin of mine who lived in Kansas City. I don't think she ever forgave me.

"Then, I was on the *Crown*, editor, like you. Mother Celeste was the advisor in those days, and she would change words in my column or leave words out or change sentences around. Whatever it took to ruin it. I couldn't believe it. She did it week after week. Why would a nun, a best-selling author, be jealous of a high school girl writing a column in the school paper? She would edit my stuff and ruin it on purpose.

"Then, when I was in the novitiate, I was the table reader. Mother Celeste would correct my pronunciation of words and make me do penance in the refectory. We used to have to do things like kneel in the center of the room with our arms outstretched, or kiss the floor, or beg for bread. Medieval stuff like that. Horrible. Embarrassing. She would make me do that stuff all the time. Once she told me I mispronounced the word 'interloper.' She made me read the same thing the next night, and say 'in*ter*loper.' I know it sounds ridiculous. Petty to even remember all that old stuff. In the convent, little things become enormous."

"It's not petty," I said. "It's horrible. She was horrible. But I can't figure out the leap from that kind of nasty stuff to getting me down here to accuse you of murder."

"Last May, she got sick. We could see that the end was near. The doctor told us Mother wouldn't live another three months. The council decided to relieve her of responsibility. She went into a rage. She was furious at me in particular. She didn't like it that I had been elected to the council in the first place. She tried to prevent me from being first councilor. The first councilor is always the assistant superior, but Mother said the superior should have the right to name her own assistant. There was a big to-do over that. But the council said no. I had been elected, and I was assistant. She could like it or lump it. She acted as if I didn't exist. She hid everything from me. The assistant is supposed to take care of temporal matters. Money. In the old days, the assistant was called the cellarer—the one who bought things for the cellar—wine, staples, whatever was needed. But Mother Celeste wouldn't let me get near the books. I asked her a few times if I could take a look at the books, and she flew into a tantrum.

"Then in May, we took away her responsibilities. We told the bishop, and he agreed with what we were doing. Mother was too sick to do anything about it. The other councilors called me in Kansas City a few days later and told me to come down here. They had been looking at the books, and they wanted me to see them. There were bills piled up. People were sending dunning notices, demanding money. Doctors. Stores. I looked at the books going all the way back. There were terrible discrepancies. When I asked Mother Celeste about it, she flew into a rage and accused me of all kinds of things. She said she'd make me sorry. It was that night I had a heart attack.

"I felt ashamed of myself. There's something shameful about being sick. I felt I had brought it on myself for not being more understanding. Mother Celeste had been superior for sixty years. Naturally, she was territorial. She had written every check and made every decision for sixty years. Why would I move in so thoughtlessly and think she would hand over the reins without a fight? Was there something deep inside me that made me do it more harshly than necessary? Was I paying her back for the ruined editorials and the penances in the refectory? And maybe for what she did to Sister Barbara?''

''What kind of discrepancies?''

''Frances, I know you'll be discreet. There's money missing. A lot of money. All the money. I don't know what we're going to do. I'm thinking that after the funeral, when I have time to go through her papers, I'll get an auditor in here and figure out where we stand.''

Another group of visitors arrived. There was a crowd on the porch now, nuns and visitors, sitting in the sun, talking and laughing.

''You're the official superior now?''

''Until we hold an election. August.''

''Are you going to be okay during these three days?''

''I'll be fine. I'm feeling so relieved right now. I was thinking Mother had fallen or even jumped off the porch because of the meeting. Because of me. I was starting to feel that her saying I was a murderer was like a prophecy. That I had *become* a murderer. That I had murdered her. Do you know what I mean? It's terrible, but I'm happy to learn someone else killed her. I thought *I* had.''

''If anyone was a murderer, it was Mother Celeste. She murdered Sister Barbara by driving her to suicide. Why was she so determined to keep her in the convent against her will?''

TWENTY

THERE WERE CARS parked next to mine in such a way that I couldn't move it out. I walked uptown. It was eleven o'clock when I knocked on Winnie's screen door.

"Come in," she called. She hurried into the front hall. "I've been in the kitchen making plans for tomorrow night."

"I can come back this afternoon, Mrs. Ross."

"No, Frances. Let's talk now." She led me up the stairs. "Let's go upstairs. Connie, who helps me, is in the kitchen. We can talk in Barbara's room."

The round tower at the corner of the house was three stories high. On the first floor, the room in the tower was the library. Pauline's old room was in the second story of the tower. The top story, higher than the rest of the house, contained the circular room where Barbara Ross had spent her girlhood. It was a shrine to her memory. Her school books, yearbooks, stuffed animals, dolls, and ice skates were on the shelves. On the walls were pictures: the twins blowing out two candles on a cake, four-year-old twins in pajamas standing by a forties kind of Christmas tree, the twins as first communicants, Barbara on ice skates, Barbara with various dogs, Barbara's graduation from St. Ad's. There were two pictures of Barbara on her Reception Day. In one she wore her bride's dress. In the second she was dressed in her new habit with a white veil and a crown of roses. There was the same Profession Day picture that had appeared in the *Herald* above her obituary. There was a picture of Barbara and Sharon in white habits. Barbara was very thin. Her cincture hung low on her hip like a gun belt.

Through the curved windows in the tower, I could see the town square and Braddock Brothers across the street. To the east, I could see the dome of St. Adelaide's.

Winnie said, "Did you know Barbara?"

"Only by sight. She was very beautiful. I can still remember the way she walked."

"If I could turn back the clock."

What would you have done differently? I wanted to ask Winnie that question, but somehow I couldn't. I watched Eddie Braddock leave the bank, and walk across the street to Harley's. "Mrs. Ross, when you talked to Mother Celeste Saturday night, how did she seem?"

"Like her old self. When I heard the next morning that she was dead, I couldn't believe it. The night before, she was sitting up in a chair writing. She had her glasses on, and she spoke so calmly. She was like she was thirty years ago."

"What did she say?"

"She said we had all made mistakes with Barbara. She said if we could forgive each other, God would forgive us. She wanted to see Tommy last. She had her prayerbooks on the table. I think she wanted to go to confession."

"Tommy went in last?"

"We all took turns. I think we all wanted to go in and scream at her. I know I did." Winnie sat down on the bed. She picked up a doll that was sitting against the pillow and stroked its long, blonde hair. "This is

Sparkle Plenty," she said. "Barbara never played with dolls."

"You wanted to scream at her?"

"I just wanted to scream, period. You're Pauline's age."

"Yes."

"I'll tell you something that you won't understand. As you get older, you feel less. You're in the last stage of life where you'll feel anything really strongly. Enjoy it. Deep feelings. Good and bad. The feelings I had last night—rage, grief, sorrow—were the strongest feelings I've had in twenty years or more. You don't understand what I'm talking about. Part of the joy of life is that we don't realize how fast it's going. My daughter killed herself because I was too cowardly to stand up to my husband."

I waited, but she was finished. Was she telling me she hadn't killed Mother Celeste because she really didn't give a damn about anything anymore? I saw Peter Ross leave the *Herald* office and start across the square.

"Mr. Ross is coming."

"I'll go down and tell Connie he's on his way." She stood up, replaced the doll, and carefully smoothed the place on the bed where she had been sitting.

As I was leaving the house, Peter Ross was coming up the walk. He touched his hat brim. "Good morning, Ms. Finn," he said.

"Good morning, Mr. Ross."

I went to Harley's. Eddie Braddock was standing at the cash register paying for his carryout order. "Ms. Finn," he said. "I've been wondering when we can talk. We have a debt to settle."

I had intended to cancel the debt since I hadn't done what Mother Celeste had wanted me to do, but I had a few questions for Eddie. "We could talk this afternoon if you like."

He looked at his Rolex. "Well, I'm on the run as you can imagine. I've got to get back out to St. Adelaide's. People expect to see me there. And I've got a bank to run. I've told my secretary to clear my calendar until after the funeral, but time and tide and the banking business wait for no man. I have to stop by the funeral home and get another visitors' book. I'm on my way to the bank right now. Do you want to follow me?" He put his change in his pocket, and picked up the containers of food and drink from the counter.

Someone touched my arm. It was Jack Braddock. "Did you leave anything for the rest of us, Eddie?" he said.

"I'll be in my office for the next hour, Ms. Finn," Eddie said. He left without speaking to his nephew.

Jack and I took the back booth. We couldn't talk murder in the drugstore because everyone kept coming back to talk to Jack. He was far from a social zero in the town. Finally, when things slowed down a little and the counterwoman had brought our cheeseburgers, he said, "You talked to Winnie?"

"You saw me over there?"

"I see all. I was in the top of my own tower when you were up in Winnie's."

"Winnie wasn't the one."

"On the steps?"

"Right."

"Did you ask her?"

"No."

"She goes out there all the time. Visits Sister Barbara's grave. Takes flowers."

"She does?"

"Walks out there. Winnie doesn't drive. Only Peter drives these days."

"But she wouldn't be out there in a thunderstorm."

"Probably not."

"And she was telling me her philosophy of old age. Strong passions fade."

Pauline came into Harley's. She saw us in the back booth and came back to join us. She was full of passion. "I've got the special edition coming out tomorrow. I've been out at St. Ad's all morning. They gave me wonderful pictures. It's so exciting out there. Like the old days. Like graduation or reception. Crowds of people. Every parlor jammed. People walking around outside, up and down the long drive. Everyone is having a ball. There's no weeping or gnashing of teeth when a person ninety-six dies."

"Unless there's a will," Jack said.

"I've got to go," I said. I paid for my lunch and went outside.

Eddie's B.M.W. was parked in front of the door to the bank. I went inside. Eddie's office was just to the right of the door. From his window, he could see the square and the passing multitudes on the sidewalk. Debris from his lunch was strewn all over the room. He had my contract on his desk.

"Tear it up, Mr. Braddock," I said. "No charge."

"I should hope not. I want you to know I'm not at all happy with the course of events."

He didn't invite me to sit down. I turned to go.

"I intend to take the whole matter up with the bishop," he said.

"What matter?"

"I'm not satisfied with Sister Sharon's motivation. Why did she drag you into a matter that didn't concern you in the least? And I'm curious about why you agreed to become involved. Your methodology is unorthodox, to say the least. You permitted my aunt to believe that you would handle her instructions in confidence, and then you ran to Sister Sharon. Sister Sharon botched things so badly that my aunt had a heart attack.''

I sat down. The chair facing Eddie's desk was very uncomfortable. I thought of farmers sitting there in the cheap, uncomfortable chair, facing the light from the window, hoping for mercy.

I picked up the contract from the desk. "I'll tear this up for you. I've got my copy with me, and I'll tear that one up, too." I opened my purse carefully so Eddie couldn't see the gun. I thought about shooting him. He was sitting sideways in his chair with his little feet up on the wastebasket. I tore up both copies of the contract and dropped the pieces past his shiny loafers onto the remains of a cheeseburger.

"You're staying for the funeral?"

"Yes. I've been hired to investigate the circumstances surrounding Mother Celeste's death."

He took his feet down, and swung around in his chair. "What circumstances? Hired by whom?" He jumped up and hurried to the door. He closed the door to the little lobby and went to the window. He took a carton that held the remains of a B.L.T. and dropped it in the wastebasket. "This is more of Sister Sharon's work, I suppose."

"Jack and Al."

"Jack and Al?" Eddie sat back down at his desk. "Enlighten me. I am bewildered by this conversation."

"They can't figure out how Mother Celeste was able to walk from her bed to the porch railing Saturday night when she could hardly move to the chair without leaning on Sister Jeanette.''

"My nephews. Typical. Idle minds. Well, I'll put a stop to this." He stood up again, and came around the desk. He came very close to me and said, "They have no business butting in. And you certainly have no business aiding and abetting. If my nephews are so interested in my aunt, why didn't they show it while she was alive? I was out there every day. I have a bank to run, but I left this office every morning to go out there and entertain that poor old woman. Were my nephews ever there? Never. They have more important things to do. Like hunting. And painting barns. And pumping gas. Now they hire a detective to snoop around the town while my aunt is lying in state?" His pudgy hands were pumping the air in fury.

"You left the meeting Saturday night just as it was getting underway," I said. "Did you go to Mother Celeste's room after you left the alumnae room?"

He took a deep breath. He stepped back from me and walked over to the window again. He raised the venetian blind. He took another deep breath. "I spoke to my aunt, of course. After the bombshell Sister Sharon dropped in my lap, what else would I do?"

"How did she seem?"

"My aunt?"

"Yes."

"How do you mean?"

"When I saw her earlier, she was very weak."

"The two days you saw her were bad. Up until Friday she was as feisty as ever. We played bridge every day. She shuffled and dealt the cards like a riverboat gambler.''

"Was she in bed Saturday night?"

"No. She was sitting in her chair. Very calm. She could have walked across the porch easily. In fact, she wanted to while I was there. I talked her into staying put. Is this what my nephews have hired you to do?"

"Yes."

"Al and Jack are grown men and they act like children. Spoiled brats. My brother spoiled them rotten. My mother always said those two had no sense of what it means to be a Braddock, any more than their mother had. I'll put a stop to this. An old woman has a heart attack while watching a storm. Something she loved to do. Everyone knows that. Except, apparently, my nephews. And she falls over the railing. Dead before she hits the ground. I hope when my time comes, it's as quick and easy as that."

"Someone was seen on the steps Saturday night. About the time Mother Celeste died. That person may have seen her fall."

"Ms. Finn, I'm trying to be patient. My aunt had regard for you as she had for all the old St. Adelaide's girls. But I'm a busy man. My nephews have problems, and they've decided to use you to help them try to get Uncle Eddie's goat. They've been at me for years, but this could very well be the straw that breaks the camel's back. I'll speak to Al and Jack, and if they don't back off, I'll speak to Randy Hermann. I suggest to you that you go back to Kansas City. Disentangle yourself from my nephews' schemes. If you don't take my advice, I'll ask Chief Hermann to explain to you why you should. There's nothing to investigate. Ask the doctor. Ask the police chief. Now I've got to go. I'll tell Al and Jack myself that this little game is over. I will not have my aunt's funeral turned into a circus by those two clowns."

I stood up. I could see Peter Ross crossing the square on his way back to the *Herald*. Eddie saw him, too. He said, "There's a special edition of the paper coming out to honor my aunt's memory. It will make a nice souvenir for the people coming to the funeral. Did you say someone was seen on the steps? Who was seen? And by whom?"

"I don't know. That's what I'm trying to find out." I left. Was I afraid of Randy Hermann? Maybe. Cops, even in a little town like Braddock, Kansas, can get rough when they want to. Who held the mortgage on Randy Hermann's house? The Bank of Braddock? Eddie Braddock was a powerful man in his little corner of Kansas. He knew the town's secrets and the convent's. I was an interloper from Missouri.

TWENTY-ONE

IN THE *Herald* office, Pauline was at her word processor, typing furiously. Peter Ross was at his word processor, typing slowly. There were old photographs laid out on the counter in a montage. Pauline waved and kept on typing. Peter Ross, ever courtly, stood and greeted me. "Good afternoon, Ms. Finn."

"Good afternoon, Mr. Ross. I can see you're busy. I was wondering if I could talk to you sometime."

He looked at Pauline.

She said, "This goes out at three, Dad. Nothing to do after that."

"Will you come to the house at three-thirty?"

"Yes."

Pauline got up and came to the counter. "Aren't these beautiful?" she asked.

There was a sepia picture of baby Celeste Walsh standing barefoot on her mother's lap. There was a picture of her holding hands with one of the founders. She was four years old and dressed in a black uniform with an enormous bow at the back of her long curls. There she was at age eight with a donkey. There she was with her classmates carrying a thick garland of flowers on graduation day. There was a picture of Celeste and her sister Stella dressed in Greek tunics, dancing by the pergola. In a picture of Sister Celeste on her Reception Day, she stood with her companion in religion in front of the old convent. There was snow on the ground, and the two new novices held copies of the rule in their hands.

"That other novice never made vows," Pauline said. "When the two of them were about to make vows, that one stepped back from the altar. She couldn't go through with it. Only Mother Celeste made vows. The other one left the convent. Isn't that romantic?"

"Very. Are you putting that in your story?"

"Of course. Everything. I've had most of it written for months now. Ready to go when she died. The paper comes back from the printer tonight at nine. What are you doing for dinner?"

"Harley's. Or the A and W. Join me?"

"Sure. Six? I'll pick you up."

I walked back to St. Ad's. It was hot, and I took my time.

The campus was full of people. If I squinted, the middle-aged women walking around were academy girls. The old nuns lined up on the porch in their wheelchairs were the strong, young teachers they once had been.

The car that had been blocking mine was gone. I got in my car and phoned for messages. I made a few phone calls. I recorded a few ideas. I went into the old convent. Zita was in the infirmary. "We've moved back over here," she said.

"We have?"

"I put your stuff back in your room. There are so many people coming, that I had to make some more beds on the third floor. If anyone comes in, he'll have to pass through a crowd to get to you."

I went upstairs. There were names in the slots on the doors now. Mine said, Miss Frances Finn, just like when I was in school.

At three-thirty, I drove back uptown. The Rolls was parked in the driveway of the Rosses' house, and Peter was in the front yard. "My wife is resting," he said. "I thought we could talk in the backyard."

"I won't keep you," I said. "I just wanted to ask you how Mother Celeste seemed Saturday night."

We walked behind the garage to a little garden surrounded by a wire fence. Morning glories, a moonvine, sweet peas, hollyhocks each had a side of the yard. The center was filled with roses. We sat on a bench by the birdbath.

"She seemed detached. Unconcerned about what she had done."

"What *had* she done?"

"To my daughter. Thirty years ago. May I ask why you're asking these questions?"

"Yes. I'm a private investigator. I don't know if Pauline told you that or not. Mother Celeste sent for me last week. She wanted me to conduct the meeting with you and your family and the community. She knew she was about to die, and she wanted to clear up any doubts that might remain about Sister Barbara's death. I told Sister Sharon what Mother Celeste had asked me to do, and Sister Sharon said she would prefer to preside at the meeting herself."

"They couldn't let Barbara rest in peace."

"After the meeting, Mother Celeste died. Jack and Al Braddock have asked me to find out from you and Mrs. Ross and Pauline and Father Ross how Mother Celeste seemed to you after the meeting. She must have been very agitated to find the strength to walk from her chair across the porch like that."

"She wasn't agitated in the least. My wife was agitated. Mother Celeste was detached. Indifferent. She listened to what I had to say, but she said nothing. Platitudes. Forgive. We should all forgive.''

"What time was it when you talked to her?"

"Eight-thirtyish. Pauline went in first. My wife went in next. It was getting dark. Starting to rain. I walked down to Barbara's grave and read her letter there. I could barely see to read. When it started to rain, I went back up to the motherhouse. My wife was in the front parlor, crying. I went in to see Mother Celeste."

"She was in her chair?"

"Watching the rain. Writing a letter. She started talking about the elm trees. I was not interested in discussing Dutch elm disease with the woman who drove my daughter to suicide."

"What did your daughter say in her note?"

He glared at me, but I didn't care. What could he do? If he didn't like my question, he could lump it. He was an old man. By the time he got out of his chair to strangle me, I would have my gun drawn. By the time he got his hands around my throat, I'd have pulled the trigger. His brains would be spread all over the garden.

"She said Mother Celeste was going to put her in an insane asylum. She said she had told Mother Celeste she wanted to leave the convent. She wanted to get a dispensation from her vows. She said Mother Celeste told her she would never allow it. She would put her in an insane asylum first. If only my daughter had come to me."

What a liar. I looked into his cruel eyes and shivered. On a July afternoon in Kansas, sitting in the sun, I was shivering. "You never knew before last night that your daughter had committed suicide?"

"Mother Celeste told us Barbara had a cerebral hemorrhage."

"Did you think to have an autopsy?"

"I suggested it, of course, but Mother Celeste was opposed to the idea. I was too upset to insist. Mother Celeste told us the doctor had assured her it was unnecessary. A cerebral hemorrhage was the typical outcome of Barbara's disease. She had a tropical virus that eventually reaches the brain. Did you know my daughter, Ms. Finn?"

"I knew who she was."

"Barbara was not the type to allow herself to be held prisoner. She was like me. I carried a cyanide pellet throughout the war. I was not about to be taken alive by the Japs."

"You told Mother Celeste you felt her threat about the mental hospital drove Sister Barbara to suicide?"

"I did."

"What did she say?"

"Nothing. Platitudes. God doesn't blame a suicide. No one can commit suicide rationally. Therefore, it's not a mortal sin. She said she believes Barbara is in heaven. I believe so, too. I feel her very close to me sometimes. I believe she's a powerful advocate in heaven."

"How long did you stay with Mother Celeste?"

"Ten minutes at the most. There was nothing to say. She killed my daughter. Our family was destroyed when Barbara died. We've never recovered. That's Mother Celeste's fault. In a way, I'm glad I didn't know what happened at the time. I'm glad Sister Sharon hid Barbara's notes. The knowledge that I could have saved my daughter if I had just known what she was going through would have been too much all those years ago. My wife and I are old now. We know what people do, the kinds of thoughtless decisions people make, what terrible repercussions the most inconsequential actions can have. There's no going back.''

"So you left Mother Celeste's room at nine?"

"About that.''

"How did she seem?''

"Detached. As I said.''

"I mean physically.''

"Strong. Leaning forward in her chair. Gesturing with her hands. Al and Jack asked you to talk to me about this?''

"Yes.''

"Why can't they come across the street and ask me themselves?''

"Someone was seen on the convent steps Saturday night. Very late. Sunday morning, really. One o'clock. That person may have seen Mother Celeste fall.''

"Who saw someone on the steps?''

"I did. I couldn't tell who it was.''

"It must have been Mother Celeste. Maybe she walked down there, and had a heart attack. There's no proof she fell over the railing.''

"That's what we're trying to find out. Did Father Ross go in to see Mother Celeste after you came out?''

"I don't know. I suppose so. I got Winnie from the parlor and brought her home. I don't know where Tom was. Still around. I think his car was still there.''

In Peter Ross's eyes, I could see the cruelty of every father of every dysfunctional family. He was every alcoholic, every child molester, every wife beater, every religious fanatic, every liar, every destroyer of a daughter. "Did you go back out to St. Ad's after you brought Mrs. Ross home?" On foot? Did you kill the old woman who conspired with you to keep your daughter in the convent? As if he would answer.

"No. Winnie and I sat up for a while talking about our daughter. Then we went to bed."

I couldn't think of any more questions for him. I thanked him and left.

I drove back to St. Ad's. I parked on the street behind the old convent so no one could block me in. I went up to the dorm. Zita had put a notice on the bulletin board: "Supper for guests in the girls' dining room at six." Someone else had written under the notice, "Cocktails on the old convent porch at five-thirty."

The doors to the rooms were open, and three or four of them were occupied. There were suitcases on beds, hairdryers, radios, all kinds of stuff old boarding school girls would know to bring. A woman stepped out of a room and introduced herself. I shook hands with her and told her my name and my class year. "We're having cocktails on the porch at five-thirty," she said. "Everyone's invited."

"Thank you." I went to the library and checked out *Walsh's Creek.* I went back upstairs to sit on the fire escape and read and watch the activity on the campus below.

TWENTY-TWO

BY THE TIME Pauline arrived, the cocktail party was in full swing. I went downstairs when I saw her drive up the long drive. She had to park on the lilac field.

"Let's eat here," she said.

The women on the porch had a bag of ice, plastic cups, and bottles of premixed Margaritas and Daiquiris. They poured drinks for Pauline and me. We stood on the steps talking to them. It was like school days, except that in those days, we just sat around talking in the half hour before supper. No alcoholic beverages were served.

Across the campus, we saw a nun step out onto the motherhouse porch and sound the clacker. That was the signal for the Angelus. We walked over to the north door, and went down to the dining room. The dining room was below the alumnae room, and was the same size. It was furnished with round tables for six. The familiar smell in the room brought back memories of meals eaten in the past with schoolmates from all over America—North, Central, and South.

The nuns were eating in the dining room with the guests. Sister Sharon led the Angelus and grace. At the end of the prayer, just like in the old days, the burst of conversation began. A woman at our table recognized Pauline. "You're Barbara Ross's sister, aren't you?"

"Yes, did you know her?"

They had been classmates. Another woman, a year or two younger, had come from Texas to attend the funeral. "Do you girls remember my sister, Hortensia Reál?"

"We were just talking about her yesterday," I said. "She used to smoke Gauloises."

Hortensia was married, the woman said. She lived in Guadalajara.

A priest at our table told Pauline he would be going to Tom Ross's party later in the evening.

After supper, just as after supper in school days, everyone went outside to stroll around the long drive, down to the pergola, across to the grotto, down to the gate, back up to the statue. At the statue, people were looking at the place where Mother Celeste's body had lain. I could see that the white hair was still attached to the base of the statue. It moved in the air current.

Pauline said, "Come uptown and wait for the paper with me? It'll be back from the plant at nine."

We drove uptown and went into Deanie's Taproom. Deanie's was a typical Kansas bar, long and narrow, wood floor, uncomfortable booths, bags of pork rinds and popcorn in racks on the bar, slow dancing in the rear, a jukebox with country music on it. Pauline and I ordered Cokes.

I said, "What did you say to Mother Celeste Saturday night?"

"Nothing, really. What could I say to someone about to die? Too bad you helped my dad drive my sister to suicide?"

"You blame your dad?"

"He killed Barb as sure as if he stuck a knife in her."

"You went in first to see Mother Celeste?"

"Yes. My mother told me to go in first. She wanted to wash her face first. Am I a suspect?"

"A suspect?"

"Eddie Braddock told me Jack and Al hired you. Do you think I pushed Mother Celeste over the railing?"

"No. You talked to Eddie?"

"I went in to cash a check. Eddie was bouncing all over the bank. He told me he's going to report you to Randy Hermann. Speak of the devil."

The police chief came into Deanie's. He waved to Pauline and nodded to me.

"He doesn't seem too worried about me," I said.

"He'd only be worried if he thought you were going to make work for him. He's assuming you're not going to find out anything."

"Is there anything to find out?"

"Did someone in my dysfunctional family kill Mother Celeste? I don't know. *I* didn't. My parents? It's possible, but not probable. They've gotten to the point where they don't give a damn about anything. Tommy? I don't know. He's half nuts. He was the last one to leave."

"What time did you leave?"

"About nine. After I read Barb's note, I went in to see Mother Celeste. She told me to have Tommy come in after everyone else that wanted to talk to her was gone. I think she wanted to go to confession."

"Did she say that?"

"No, but she had her prayerbooks. And she was getting ready to write something. A list of her sins, I figured."

"How do you know she was getting ready to write something?"

"She asked me to hand her a piece of stationery from her drawer."

"What did your note from your sister say?"

"I always knew Barb would have left a note. I was

glad to get it at last. But I don't blame Sharon for not giving it to me sooner. It would have hurt too much to know for sure that Barb killed herself. The way it was, I could halfway believe the cerebral hemorrhage story. I read all about her disease in medical books, and it could have been true. Now, I'm old enough to handle it. It's not going to make me kill myself to know my sister killed herself. In a way, I have to admire her. She got out. She was determined to get out, and she did. It's too bad it had to be that way, but she couldn't figure out any other way. If only Tommy had had the guts to help her. I've seen enough suffering to know that suicide is a legitimate option. If it were now, she'd know what to do. Just walk out. Tell Mother Celeste and my dad to go fuck themselves. But in nineteen sixty-five she didn't know. Sharon did the right thing. I'm going to thank her.''

"I remember once you told me Sharon was your favorite nun."

"She was yours, too, wasn't she?"

"Yes."

"I had her in first grade," Pauline said. "I worshiped her. I got so little attention from my parents, you wouldn't believe it. Sharon was so sweet. She was so young and so beautiful. That must have been her first year of teaching. She used to walk past my house on her way to St. George's. I would wait for her and walk to school with her. Jack Braddock would walk with us, too. Sharon would let us choose the way. One day, I'd get to choose, and the next day, Jack. I liked to go around the square. Jack liked to go by the park. Sometimes my hair wouldn't be combed. My mother worried about her own hair all the time, but she'd send me to school without combing mine. Sharon would comb it for me when we got to school. Once she braided it, and braided in some colored yarn. I looked beautiful. Like a gypsy.

"The summer before sixth grade, Barb came home for her home visit. The nuns got to go home for a visit once every five years. They had to take a companion. Barb had to bring a companion even though the convent was five blocks away. She brought Sharon. I was eleven. I loved having Sharon in my house. All to myself. Tommy was home from the seminary at the same time. He and Barb were constantly up in Barb's room. Plotting to leave. Or down in the library with my dad. Yelling. Arguing. Begging him to let them leave. It was unbelievable. Sharon spent the whole time with me. In the daytime, we'd walk out to St. Ad's, and I'd help her do stuff out there. Iron, work in the garden, print stuff, whatever she had to do. I was with her all day. In the evening, we'd walk back to my house. The yelling would still be going on. It was unbelievable. Sharon and I would go up to my room. She let me try on one of her habits, once. Remember how we always wanted to do that? She dressed me in the habit, the whole thing. I went downstairs in it to surprise my parents and Barb and Tommy. They just stared at me. They didn't laugh or react in any way. It was like I didn't exist.

"Sharon and I made pizza every night, and played Scrabble, and watched t.v. in my room. It was one of the happiest weeks of my life. Sharon in her bathrobe, sitting in my room, watching t.v." Pauline went up to the bar to get two more Cokes. When she came back to the booth, she said, "The note. Barb told me she was sorry. She told me to get away from my parents. To board at St. Ad's until I graduated. To stick close to Sharon. Then, to go away to college and graduate

school. To do whatever I wanted in life, no matter what
my parents had planned for me. My life has turned out
pretty much that way. I didn't get to board, but my
parents ignored me at home. They never tried to rule
me like they did Barb and Tom. I think my sister's
watching over me in heaven. Like a guardian angel. She
helped me go to school and journalism school. Now,
I've got my own paper. It's mine, even if Dad hangs
around. He doesn't do anything. I do what I want.''

"What ever happened to the mission in Guatemala?"

"My parents offered to keep funding it. In Barbara's
memory. Sharon didn't want to go back. A couple of
other nuns went down there for a couple of years, but
one of them got sick, too. She didn't die. Amoebic dys-
entery. They came back. I think the Adelaides turned it
over to the local people to run. It was just a hut. There
was nothing there. My parents turned the mission fund
into a scholarship fund for the academy.''

"Do you think your brother really thought Sharon
killed Barbara?"

"I never heard anything about it before Saturday
night. He's always on some weird kick. His life is one
bitter disappointment, and he tries to blame various people for various aspects.''

"What's disappointing to him?"

"He's got the usual clerical hang-ups. He's stuck
down here in Braddock. I think he pictured himself in
Rome or something. Maybe even a bishop. He just sits
out there and eats and drinks. Typical small-town
priest.''

"Is he ever violent?"

"I can't say he's violent. But the thing I've always
found oddest about my odd brother is the number of
car wrecks he gets into.''

Jack and Al Braddock walked into the bar. They saw us and came to our booth. They ordered beer and ham sandwiches. After a while, Jack asked me to dance. We went to the back of the room. Al and Pauline came back to dance. It was like high school. I hadn't danced like that for many years, wrapped closely in my partner's arms, barely moving, swaying rather than dancing.

When we got back to our booth, we saw a truck parked in front of the *Herald*. "Here's my paper," Pauline said.

TWENTY-THREE

On the front page of the special edition of the *Braddock Herald* were the pictures of Mother Celeste I had seen the day before. On the second page was a chronology of Mother Celeste's life.

Celeste Walsh was the granddaughter of Oliver Braddock who came to Kansas in 1849 from Massachusetts. He had intended to go to California to prospect for gold, but decided to put his grubstake to work in another way. He set up a store for outfitting wagon trains in Overland Park. His store was the last chance for those heading west to lay in supplies, and Oliver Braddock got rich.

He bought a piece of land fifty miles south on Walsh's Creek and platted a town. The prospectus he sent back east convinced other New Englanders to come out and join him in his venture. The town of Braddock was incorporated in 1850, and Oliver Braddock opened a bank.

He prospered, and the town prospered. On January 29, 1861, Kansas became a state, and Oliver Braddock married Martha Henry, a woman who had been waiting for his proposal since they were children. She had come out from Boston bringing her furniture and refined ways.

Their son Abraham was born in 1864, and their daughter Lorena was born in 1869. When Abraham was twelve, his parents sent him back east to be educated. Lorena stayed home with her parents. In 1891, she disappointed them by marrying a Catholic, Patrick Walsh, the son of a local farmer who had come from Ireland in 1843.

The stress over his daughter's unfortunate marriage and being locked in the safe when the Dalton boys robbed the bank killed Oliver Braddock in 1892. Martha died that same year. Abraham had graduated from Harvard in 1884 and come home to work in the bank. With his parents dead, he became president. He married a local girl, Phoebe Waite, in 1893.

Their only child, Henry, was born in 1894. That same year, Stella, the first child of Lorena and Patrick, was born on the Walsh farm outside Braddock.

That summer, three Sisters of St. Adelaide came to Kansas from Kentucky looking for a place to start a girls' school. Patrick Walsh sold them twenty acres of his farm at a good price. Lorena, though not a Catholic, invited the nuns to live in her house while their convent was being built.

The brick convent was ready by October 1895. The founders welcomed the first four students to St. Adelaide's Academy on October 7, the feast of Our Lady of Victories, a day that would afterward be celebrated at the convent as Founders Day.

Celeste Walsh, Patrick and Lorena's second child, was born on October 22, 1897. Her parents took her to the nuns' chapel the next day to be baptized.

The Walsh girls attended St. Adelaide's, starting in the class for four-year-olds. There was no parish school in Braddock in those days, so the nuns taught children of all ages at the academy. They welcomed any student who could pay and many who could not. Stella and Celeste walked across the field that separated their house from the convent every day for many years.

In school they learned music, waxwork, hairwork, embroidery, flower preserving, religion, confit making, German, china painting, and natural history.

Stella and Celeste were popular with their classmates and with the young people of the town and the surrounding farms. They went to all the socials: the picnics, pie suppers, burgoos, corn roasts, sleigh rides, taffy pulls.

"This is where the trouble begins," Jack said.

We were sitting on the sofa in Pauline's office with our copies of the *Herald* spread out on the coffee table. "What's a burgoo?" I asked.

"They used to go out in the country, and put a big kettle over a fire, and cook all day," Pauline said. "Stew. They'd throw in everything they could find or shoot. Squirrels. Chickens. Rabbits. Quail."

The Walsh girls were famous for their wit and their red hair and their beautiful smiles. No one was surprised when Henry Braddock, home from Harvard in 1914, proposed marriage to his cousin Stella.

"No one but Celeste," Al said.

Celeste entered the convent the day after Christmas. She walked across the field in the morning

and told the founders she had decided to become
a nun. The founders told her to go back home and
get her parents' permission. She went home and
ate dinner with Patrick and Lorena and her newly
engaged sister Stella. In the afternoon, she returned
to St. Adelaide's to stay.

As his daughter's dowry, Patrick Walsh forgave
the debt the nuns owed him for the corn field.

Another postulant had entered on December 16,
the feast of St. Adelaide. Celeste Walsh joined her
in the novitiate. They lived on the third floor of
the convent. They spent their days scrubbing
floors, waxing floors, polishing floors. The postulants did the laundry for the nuns and the boarders,
studied the rules and customs of the order, darned
stockings, worked in the garden, took care of the
animals, washed dishes, helped in the kitchen,
served at table, helped with the youngest boarders,
and ran errands uptown for the nuns. The nuns
observed strict cloister in those early days, and
only the postulants went out in public.

Stella Walsh and Henry Braddock were married
in 1915.

I stared at their wedding picture. "Henry looks exactly like Eddie."

That same year, Celeste Walsh received the
habit. As novices, she and her classmate spent their
days at the same tasks that had occupied them as
postulants except that now they remained in the
convent. No more trips to town.

The newlyweds, Stella and Henry, moved into

the big house east of the square with Abraham and Phoebe.

Sister Celeste made vows on December 16, 1917. Her companion in religion stepped back from the altar at the last minute. She was overcome by fear. She returned to her parents' home later that day.

Henry Braddock had enlisted in the Army a few weeks earlier. There was a picture of him and Stella with Celeste on her Profession Day. Sister Celeste had a wreath of roses on her black-veiled head. Henry was wearing puttees and a Smokey-the-Bear hat. Stella was wearing an enormous fur hat and a full-length fur coat.

"Henry looks exactly like Eddie," I said.

"Eddie the doughboy," Jack said.

The newly professed Sister Celeste was sent to Kansas City to get a college degree. The Adelaides had opened a day school for girls there the year before, and Celeste lived at their convent. She rode the streetcar every day to St. Genevieve's College. A short story she wrote about being caught in the mob downtown on Armistice Day was published in the *Kansas City Post*. She received three dollars for the piece, the first money she earned with her writing. The superior of the convent used the money to pay the coal bill.

After receiving her degree, Sister Celeste returned to Braddock to teach at the academy.

The academy was beginning to attract students from all over Kansas, Missouri, and Oklahoma. Some students came from Texas and Mexico. The community of nuns was growing as well. The founders built the X-shaped motherhouse in 1927. After the nuns moved into the new building, the original building became known as the old convent.

Lorena and Patrick Walsh would walk across the field on Sundays to visit Sister Celeste, and Stella and Henry would drive out from town in Henry's Packard.

Abraham Braddock dropped dead in his office at the bank in 1927, and Henry Braddock took over as president.

In 1928, Sister Celeste earned the master's degree she had been working toward summer after summer. She was named headmistress of the academy. That same year, Henry and Stella had their first child, Oliver.

"My dad," Jack said.

Patrick Walsh died in 1930, and Lorena followed him as quickly as her mother had followed her father. Their farm had grown over the years. Now, half the Walsh farm went to Stella, and half went to the convent as Sister Celeste's patrimony. The founders dedicated a Lourdes grotto on the campus to the memory of their first benefactors, Patrick Walsh and Lorena Braddock Walsh.

The last of the founders died in 1933, and in August of that year, Sister Celeste was elected superior.

The Bank of Braddock nearly failed that year, but somehow, Henry Braddock managed to recover. At a time when bankers in other Kansas towns were foreclosing on farms every day, informing widows that their investments had become worthless, watching old friends die of shame or self-inflicted bullet wounds, Henry Braddock managed to keep the bank and the town alive. Throughout the depression, he carried farmers and business owners who would have lost everything without him. In 1938, to the surprise of Henry and Stella who were no longer young, their second child, Edgar, was born.

"Eddie was an idiot," Jack said. "My dad told me he didn't learn to talk until he was five years old."

A few weeks after the birth of her second grandson, old Phoebe died. Now Stella was mistress of the big house at last. Nearly every afternoon, she pushed her pudgy baby in his big black buggy out to the convent. She and Mother Celeste would sit on the convent porch on summer afternoons. Little Eddie loved his aunt, and she loved him.

Oliver Braddock decided to go to K.U. instead of Harvard. After graduation, he got a job at a funeral parlor in Kansas City. In 1949, he married his employer's daughter, Judy Moore.

"They had to get married," Al said. "Mom was pregnant with me."

Mother Celeste finished her doctorate in 1949. As her thesis, she had written a book about her early life on the farm. Her advisor passed her manuscript to a publisher in New York, and *Walsh's Creek* was published. The book was a bestseller in 1950. It was dedicated to Edgar Braddock.

When Judy was pregnant with Jack, Oliver had to go to Korea. Stella invited her daughter-in-law to come live with her in Braddock. Henry was at the bank all day, and Eddie was in school, and Stella was lonely.

Judy brought baby Al to Braddock, and moved into the big house with Stella and Henry and Eddie. Jack was born soon after.

When Oliver returned from Korea, Stella persuaded him to remain in Braddock. Stella offered him use of the big house on the square for his own funeral home. Oliver and Judy agreed to stay in Braddock, and raise their boys there.

Henry and Stella and Eddie moved out to the Walsh farmhouse. The town had grown so much that the farmhouse, like the convent, was now at the edge of town, connected to the water supply, electricity, and sewer.

Henry and Stella and Eddie would walk across the field on summer evenings. Mother Celeste would be sitting outside with the nuns at recreation. Eddie loved listening to Mother Celeste's stories. Sometimes Henry and Stella would sing for the nuns. Henry played the ukelele while they sang the old songs.

The community was growing. The profession classes now contained as many as ten sisters. Mother Celeste wanted to open a house of studies. She had been educated as a young nun, but that was unusual. Ordinarily, sisters were assigned to classrooms without degrees or credentials. They would teach during the year, and go to school in the summer. It took years to complete degrees. But a new idea was taking hold, and Mother Celeste was in the vanguard. She was determined to build a house of studies where all newly professed sisters would go. The sisters would graduate from college before being assigned to teach.

Judy Braddock, Al and Jack's mother, died in 1956.

In 1958, Mother Celeste realized her dream. With Henry, Stella, and Eddie at her side, she laid the cornerstone for a juniorate in St. Louis.

There was a picture of Mother Celeste with her foot on a shovel. Henry, looking exactly as Eddie looked now, was standing at her side. Stella and twenty-year-old Eddie were standing at her other side.

The vocation boom of the 1960s kept the juniorate bursting at the seams.

"Did Barbara ever live there?" I asked Pauline.

"Only in the summers," Pauline said. "She started to teach at St. George's right after profession. I think my parents and Mother Celeste wanted to keep her here during the year. Keep an eye on her."

In the late sixties, when the exodus from religious life began, the junior nuns were the first to go. Vocations dried up. The house of studies was sold.

In 1973, Henry Braddock died, and Eddie took over the bank. In 1977, the nuns closed the academy. Stella died in 1980, and was laid to rest next to Henry, her cousin and husband.

Eddie Braddock never married. He continued to live with Stella in the Walsh farmhouse until her death. After her death, he lived there alone.

Oliver Braddock died in 1981. His sons, Al and Jack, took over the funeral home.

In 1983, to celebrate her fiftieth anniversary as superior, Mother Celeste arranged a journey of reconciliation. She rented a bus, and took fifteen Kansas Adelaides with her to Kentucky. The two communities of nuns, separated by nearly a century of bad feelings, embraced. Mother Celeste and her nuns spent a week at Mount Adelaide in Louisville. They visited the convent graveyard and prayed at the graves of the five Adelaides who came from Germany in 1844, nuns Mother Celeste had heard about from the founders of the Kansas convent. The Kentucky nuns gave the Kansas nuns relics of the German pioneers and copies of the community chronicle. They gave them a copy of the wartime diary of Sister Hedwig, an Adelaide famous for nursing the wounded soldiers of both armies at Shiloh.

Back in Braddock, Mother Celeste, nearly ninety, used the material from Kentucky to write her second book, *Decades of Joy*. She continued to publish articles in historical journals. She wrote for the *Alumnae Bulletin*. She continued to guide the dwindling and aging community with a firm hand.

Around 1990, Mother Celeste began to slow down.

Mother Celeste's long life ended when she wandered from her room to the convent porch during a thunderstorm. She suffered a fatal heart attack while the rain fell and the wind blew. She fell over the banister, and her body lay all night behind the statue of St. Adelaide. Mother Celeste had always loved thunderstorms. She tells in *Walsh's Creek* how Patrick and Lorena and Stella would run for the cyclone cellar when a twister appeared in the summer sky. Celeste would be the last one to seek shelter. She would stand at the cellar door until the last possible minute, tasting the rain, facing the wind, watching the storm come from the west.

"Fabulous," I said. "Pauline, it's beautiful."

"How did you pull all this together so fast?" Al asked.

"I've had it ready for a while. Most of it. I knew she'd be dying sooner or later, so I've had the memorial edition more or less ready. I just filled in the details this morning."

The third page was full of black-edged ads from local businesses. "I got the ads last May," Pauline said to Al. "Yours is here."

The fourth page had reprints of items from old *Heralds* about Mother Celeste, the Braddocks, the Walshes, and St. Adelaide's.

"It's wonderful, Pauline," Jack said.

"Beautiful." I asked Pauline and Jack and Al to sign the paper for me. Pauline wrote her signature on the masthead. Al signed his name on the Braddock Brothers Funeral Home ad. Jack wrote below a picture of the old convent bell: "When you cast your eyes upon this bell, remember one who rang it well!"

TWENTY-FOUR

PAULINE FILLED the box outside the *Herald* with copies of the special edition. We put another stack in the trunk of her car to take to St. Adelaide's. "Let's go to my brother's party," she said.

It was eleven o'clock. The visiting priests and several parishioners were in the backyard of Tom Ross's rectory. Tom welcomed us and led us to the food. The women of the parish had brought fried chicken, barbecued ribs, ham, coleslaw, potato salad, marshmallow salad, various chow chows, and several pies. The priests had finished eating, and were concentrating on drinking.

We sat down with the priests. Jack and Al joined their discussion of sports, and Pauline and I ate pie and drank coffee. After a while, we went inside. Pauline started cleaning up her brother's kitchen. I asked her where the bathroom was. Through the bedroom.

Barbara's last letter to her twin was on his bedside table. I took it with me into the bathroom. I locked the door and read it.

November 30, 1965

To my other,

I won't ask you to forgive me, because I know you won't. Any more than I would forgive you if you left me behind. I won't ask you to understand. I know you do. You understand me as well as I understand myself. All our thoughts, all our memories, all our heartbeats. Remember our invisible friends. Mary Fennell? The Yodeler? Remember listening to the radio? Corliss Archer? The Great Gildersleeve? Baby Snooks? Froggy the Gremlin? Remember our tent?

You get my last words on earth, Mitoo. When I finish this letter, I will turn off my light and close my eyes. When I open them again, I will see you. It's eternity, isn't it? You're there already, and I'm there. We came from there, and we're always there.

Mama and Daddy were here all afternoon. I tried to make them understand. Hopeless. After they left, Mother Celeste told me she had talked to them, and they agree with her. They want to put me in St. Michael's. I can't go there, Tom.

How can a psychiatrist pretend that this life is sane? How can he say I should be hospitalized, tranquilized, turned into a zombie because I want to leave a place where conversation is forbidden? Where silence is a virtue? Where I'm expected to eat every meal in silence sitting between the same two people for the rest of my life? Where I'm supposed to be a teacher, but forbidden to read what I choose to read? Where friendship is suspect? Where love is reserved for spirits? You know how it is. Everyone knows, but everyone pretends. Who's insane?

I told Mother Celeste I would kill myself if she didn't arrange for me to get a dispensation from my vows. She grabbed me and shook me and screamed at me. "Don't crucify me!" She kept screaming that at me.

I'm sick, Tommy. The doctor down there in G. gave me the wrong medicine. I know there's something growing in my brain. I can feel it, and in my dreams, I can see it. You wouldn't want me to go on with this pain. I think Mother Celeste is trying to keep me in the convent so she can keep my dowry.

Please take care of Pauline. Make sure she has the right clothes, and gets to go to college. Take care of yourself, Tommy, Mitoo, my other. Always witoo. Witoo, witoo.

Barbara

I flushed the toilet. I looked in Tommy Ross's medicine cabinet. A few packs of razor blades, deodorant, floss, toothpaste. No pills.

I put the letter back on his nightstand.

Pauline was loading the dishwasher. Jack came inside. "Getting tired?" he asked.

"I never stay up this late," I said.

"I'll drive you back," Pauline said. "Is Al ready to go?"

He was ready. We got in Pauline's car. Jack drove, and Pauline and Al got in the back seat. "Shall I go the long way?" Jack asked. He lit a joint and passed it around. He drove out to a roadhouse in the country. The parking lot was full, and the tavern was full. A band was playing, and people were dancing. I noticed Randy Hermann in the crowd on the dance floor. "Doesn't anybody in this town sleep?" I asked.

"They're afraid if they go to sleep, they'll never wake up," Pauline said. She and Al headed straight for the dance floor.

Jack and I sat down. "What happened to the money?" I asked.

"The Braddock money?" Jack wasn't surprised at my question.

"You said your grandmother played a trick with her will."

"Stella never got over being pissed at my dad for marrying my mom. My mom was an alcoholic. Back then, it was more or less okay. Everybody drank. Everybody had bars in their houses. Remember that? The high fifties. Bar sets and fancy tools and shakers. Cocktails and highballs. But mom went a little bit overboard. My mom more or less drank herself to death. I don't know why. Just the typical fifties depression that took a lot of people.

"My grandmother, Stella, inherited the bank when my grandfather, Henry Braddock, died. She had inherited half the Walsh farm when her parents died. The good half. Mother Celeste got the side with the rocks and gullies. Grandma got the side with the house and the barns and the trees and the best land.

"Grandma owned other stuff, too. The house on the square, for one thing. We lived in it, but she never put it in my dad's name. He always assumed she'd leave it to him when she died. Along with half of everything else. He thought his mother would divide everything down the middle. Half for Eddie and half for Ollie.

"But when she died, it turned out she left the bank to Eddie, the house in town to Eddie, the various other stuff to Eddie, and nothing to my dad. Ollie got zip. Ollie got screwed for marrying a girl Grandma didn't like thirty years earlier. She had carried the grudge all those years. The Braddocks don't age well. She was pissed because he didn't just stay with her like Eddie did and never get married.

"In her will, Grandma divided her half of the Walsh

farm in four parts. The part with the house went to Eddie. Another part, a cultivated part, went to the convent. The last two parts, the worst parts, went to Al and me.''

"Eddie got the funeral home?"

"Well, he got the house. The business was my dad's. Eddie let us keep living there. We paid rent. My dad died a year after Grandma died. So Al and I inherited the business. We still paid rent on the house to Eddie. But the ironic thing happened a year later. In eighty-three. When the interstate came through, the land they most wanted, had to have in fact, was the part of the farm Grandma left Al and me. Also the part the convent got. So Al and I came into some money after all. We bought the house from Eddie. That's when we fixed it up.

"I'm a rich man, Frances. I've always had a green thumb when it comes to getting money. Even before Grandma died, I paid my way through college by growing ditchweed on the farm. Down by the creek where nobody went, I grew pot. Actually my great-great-grandpa, John Walsh, grew pot. I just harvested it. Hemp. It was a cash crop in his day. Braddock had a big rope works then. That long, skinny, brick building by the railroad track? That was the old rope works. Big business in the Civil War. The Braddock Rope Works supplied rope for the Union Army. Patrick Walsh, my great-grandpa, kept it up. He raised hundreds of bales of hemp on the farm every year. After he died, they turned to corn and alfalfa. But down there by the creek, the marijuana still grows tall. It's not great dope, but it's good enough. It paid my way through K.U. No one ever goes down there. No one could ever figure out where I got my money. My kids can go to Harvard if they want. Like the old-time Braddocks always did.''

Pauline and Al came back from the dance floor. After an hour or so, we left. Pauline dropped Jack and Al off at the funeral home. She drove me out to St. Adelaide's. It was three o'clock when I got up to the dorm, but four women were still awake, sitting in the hall, drinking instant coffee, giggling.

I woke up at eleven Tuesday morning. I took a shower and climbed out on the fire escape to dry my hair. The campus was crowded. There were groups of people everywhere. I could see a gravedigger preparing Mother Celeste's grave.

A black Mercedes drove up the long drive and parked in front of the motherhouse. Four priests got out, including an old one who walked a little bit ahead of the others. The bishop, I presumed.

Someone knocked on my door. I climbed back in the room and opened the door. Zita was there with my breakfast tray. Coffee, convent bread, marmalade. ''I didn't have any peanut butter,'' she said. ''Those girls down on the second floor ate it all last night.''

''This is perfect. Thank you.''

''I brought you a copy of the *Herald*, too.'' Pauline had left a stack in the hall downstairs when she brought me back.

''Thanks.'' I opened it, and began to read the saga of the Braddocks and the Walshes once again.

Zita poured coffee for me. The tray and the dishes were cheap. Where was the beautiful old silver service she used to bring to our rooms when we were sick? A wave of emotion rushed through me. So many feelings had been competing in my heart and my head. I had been trying to be a detective, calm, unrattled by danger, unmoved by death, but seeing Zita pour my coffee turned back my clock. I was an adolescent girl again, emotions at the ready. I wanted to put my arms around this little nun in her old-fashioned habit.

She felt me wanting to hug her. She said, "It's nice having you here. It's just like before. And all the other girls." She patted my arm.

She went to the window and looked out. "I've got to go," she said. "I've got a house full at Father's. A couple of the nuns from Kansas City are over there cooking dinner for the priests. I've got to get over there to make sure they find everything."

After she left, I opened *Walsh's Creek.* I wanted to read the chapter again where the heroine's sister gets engaged. Mother Celeste had not used her religious title on the book, and there was no picture of her on the cover. No one would know Celeste Walsh was a nun. The story was fiction, supposedly. The book ends with the wedding of the handsome bridegroom and the red-haired bride. There is no mention of the younger sister's entering the convent, only of her heartbreak when the man she loved chose another.

Celeste Walsh had been in love with Henry Braddock. One night on a sleigh ride, they sat side by side under the same blanket. As the horse pulled the sleigh across the snowcovered fields, and harness bells jingled, and millions of stars lit the winter sky, Celeste waited for Henry to speak. Instead, the next night, walking back across the field from midnight mass at the convent chapel, he proposed to her sister.

TWENTY-FIVE

AT NOON, I went over to the motherhouse. A nun was standing on the porch sounding the clacker. The doors to the chapel were open, and I could hear Sharon intoning the Angelus. The nuns and the guests took it up. Next, Sharon intoned the midday prayer from the office of the dead. The nuns took it up. At the end of the prayers, the nuns and the visitors came out of the chapel and went downstairs to dinner.

Sharon came over to me. She led me to the visitors' book open on a lectern in the rotunda. "Have you signed yet?"

Thirty pages had been filled with signatures. This, apparently, was the second book because the bishop's name was on the first line of the first page. He had written his first name only, Charles, followed by a cross. The next person to sign on the first page, a priest, had skipped a line. Should I write my name on the blank line after the bishop's? Maybe just my first name. "I'll sign later," I said. "I have to think of a clever saying first."

"Come down to the refectory with me?" Sharon asked. "Or go to the dining room? We're serving four dinners today. The bishop and his people are in the bishop's dining room. The order priests are over at Father's house."

"I've got to talk to you," I said. "Are you going to have any time this afternoon?"

"I've got to lie down at one. Then, I'm meeting with

the bishop at three. We've got vespers at five. I can see you at four-thirty. I hope the bishop doesn't keep me longer than an hour. What's going on? Have you found out anything?''

"I want to take a look at the books."

"The books?''

"You said money is missing. I want to look at the convent accounts. Would that be possible?''

"What are you thinking?''

"Follow the money. The lesson of Watergate.''

The rotunda emptied as the last of the nuns and guests went downstairs. Sharon led me to the office. Sister Jeanette was sitting at a little table reading the special edition of the *Herald*. She had finished taking dinner trays to the nuns in the infirmary, and now she was watching the office. Sharon told her I would be taking a look at the ledgers.

Sharon unlocked the old-fashioned safe and took out a stack of books. "You'll think the bookkeeping is amazingly crude,'' she said. She put the books on a table. "You can look through these. Aren't you hungry?''

"No, thanks. I just had breakfast."

Sharon left. The first entry in the first ledger recorded the down payment of twenty dollars the founders made to Patrick Walsh for the corn field which became the campus of St. Adelaide's.

The copperplate hand, the ink faded to brown, the tiny sums spent on serge, flour, coal, told the story of the early years. The founders' method of bookkeeping was simple: income on the left, expenditures on the right. No line was wasted. A year might start in the middle of a page. The dates were given in numerals and saints' feasts. As each postulant entered, her dowry was recorded. The parents of one early postulant paid her expenses with a mule. Others paid with gold dust, deeds to land, cash. If a sister left the convent, her dowry was returned. The community was allowed to use the interest on a nun's patrimony during her lifetime, but not the principal. Only when she died, could the community use the principal. When the first three novices died in September 1897, the founders returned their dowries to their families.

"Those three sisters made vows on their deathbed," Jeanette explained. "But officially, they were still novices. So the founders had to give back their dowries." The expenses were itemized in the ledger for the three young victims of tuberculosis. A doctor was paid two dollars, a carpenter two dollars for their coffins, and a gravedigger seventy-five cents.

On the Feast of the Holy Innocents, 1914, Patrick Walsh forgave the debt on the land.

A windfall came to the community in 1925 when a postulant from St. Louis entered bringing as her dowry the proceeds from the sale of Mississippi riverfront real estate she had inherited.

The convent's money was kept in the Bank of Braddock from the beginning.

The academy's finances were recorded in separate ledgers. Each student's name was recorded, and her fees itemized. In the early days, students paid extra for dancing lessons. The nuns employed a dancing master who came on the train from Kansas City twice a week. The Walsh girls both took dancing lessons.

By the early twenties, the number of students had grown considerably, and with the revenue from their tuition fees, the founders built the motherhouse.

Two widows entered the community in the late twenties. Both were advanced in age and brought large inheritances to the convent's coffers. Both died in the early thirties.

Mother Celeste's big, square handwriting replaced the copperplate and the Spencerian of the founders in 1933.

Times were difficult for the Adelaides during the depression. The number of students declined, and the parents of those students who stayed often failed to pay their fees on time or at all. "We lived on rabbit," Jeanette said. "I was a novice then, and we spent all our time taking care of the rabbits. I wouldn't eat a rabbit today if you paid me."

I had heard this tale before from my teachers. They had bad memories of the depression: molasses for breakfast, rabbit for dinner, vegetable soup for supper. Seeing the purchase of fifty rabbits in Mother Celeste's handwriting made me shudder.

Mother Celeste was not the scrupulous bookkeeper the founders had been. They had recorded expenditures of even a few cents, but Mother Celeste dealt in large, round figures. They had been specific, but Mother Celeste was vague. Many of her entries had initials or abbreviations instead of complete names. The initials H.B. occurred often. Other expenditures were entered with no explanation at all. A few entries were crossed out or written over with Palmer Method spirals.

By the 1940s, the whole thing became incomprehensible. The number of students increased dramatically during the war, and the nuns doubled and then tripled the tuition fees. The electricity, coal, gas, and repair bills on the buildings increased as well. The entries in the ledger were erratic. Some things were circled, and arrows connected circles. Long arrows led sometimes from one page to the next. There were question marks, and tiny, marginal notes, and doodles on the pages. The initials H.B. appeared every two or three pages.

The number of young women entering the convent increased in the fifties, and their dowries were larger than before. I saw the amount paid by Anton Bieralski when Sharon entered and the dowry sent for Zita by the Kansas City doctor's wife. I was astonished by the enormous sum contributed by Peter Ross when Sister Barbara entered in 1957.

The number of girls from Latin American countries coming to the academy increased in the fifties. They were charged for English instruction in addition to the regular tuition.

The cost of the construction of the juniorate in St. Louis was entered as one large sum. There was no breakdown for land or subcontractors.

Walsh's Creek brought in royalty payments for ten years.

I found my own name. "Paid in full," was written by my father's name for four years. He had paid extra for my piano lessons from Sister Roberta.

I found the memorial fund invested by the Rosses when Sister Barbara died and the names of the students whose fees were paid by the interest.

In the late sixties and early seventies, more than half the nuns in the community left. Entry after entry recorded the return of dowries.

The sale of silver, antique furniture, woodwork, and pictures brought a great deal of money to the convent in the eighties. So did the sale of sections of the Walsh farm for the interstate highway.

I closed the last book. There had been no new entries for several months.

"I've been meaning to ask you something, Sister," I said to Jeanette.

"Yes?"

"Saturday night, what kind of shape was Mother Celeste in after the Rosses left?"

"She seemed better than she had for months."

"When the Rosses left, did they leave by the front door or by the door in Mother's room?"

"I don't know. I was busy putting a couple of the sisters to bed. By the time I went in to put Mother to bed, the Rosses were gone. I don't know how they left."

"Was the door in Mother's room open when you last checked on her?"

"It was closed. That was the last thing I did at night. I always locked that door. She always wanted it open during the day. She always liked it open."

"Was there a key to that door? I mean, did anyone outside have a key?"

"When they built the motherhouse, they planned that door to be there. That was always intended to be the infirmary, that room. They never dreamed there'd be a time when we'd have a whole corridor of old sick sisters. They wanted that door to the porch so a priest, or a doctor, or a sister's relatives could visit without going through the cloistered part of the house. I guess we've given out dozens of keys to that door over the years. Mother liked to have visitors. She'd been living in that room for the last two years. Before she got really sick, she moved down there. She liked to have Mr. Braddock come out to play bridge, and several women in the town used to come out to visit. Father Ross, of course. Everybody and his brother had a key to that room."

"Tom Ross?"

"He used to come visit Mother. He'd come out late at night sometimes. On his bicycle. He's a night owl, and Mother was a night owl. The two of them would be in there talking sometimes at midnight. I couldn't do it. I go to bed at ten. He'd pull the door closed when he left. It locks automatically."

"The door was open when you went in Sunday morning?"

"Yes. I usually wake up at five. The old nuns wake up early, and I like to get them started. I went in there to check on Mother, and the door was wide open. When I saw that Mother wasn't in her bed, I went straight out there. Something made me look over the railing, and there she was."

"You've seen a lot in your life."

"Yes, I have."

"You were taking care of Sister Barbara when she was sick?"

"For all the good it did."

"Were you surprised to find out she had committed suicide?"

"I'm a nurse, honey. I know that when a person is sick and in pain, you don't leave their medicine within reach. I wanted to take her medicine away from her. I knew she was addicted. I tried to explain to Mother, but Mother was more interested in not wasting the medicine. I don't blame Sister Barbara. She needed help. The doctor we had then in Braddock was an idiot. I don't know how else to say it. I had cancer a few years ago. I don't know if you knew that or not. This doctor had some crazy idea about what to do to me. I wasn't about to go along with it. I knew he didn't keep up with the literature. I told Mother Celeste I wouldn't let him touch me with a ten-foot pole. She said go along with what he said, or do without. I wanted to go to a specialist in Kansas City, but Mother Celeste said we couldn't afford it. So I did without. It was the same story with Barbara Ross. She needed help, but that doctor, he's dead now, he didn't have a clue. He said it was in her head. It *was* in her head, but not the way he thought. I'd see her rub her finger on a spot on her head like she was trying to erase the pain. Mother called in a psychiatrist from the state hospital. He and Mother and the Rosses decided to put Sister Barbara in a mental institution. I told Mother Celeste that Barbara Ross needed a real doctor. A specialist. I think she had a brain tumor.''

"You got over cancer without chemotherapy?''

"With prayer. That's all. I've got to pick up the sisters' trays, now,'' Jeanette said. "I'll be back in a couple of minutes.''

I looked through the books again. I made notes of some of the larger amounts. Where was the money? I rob banks, Willie Sutton said, because that's where the money is.

The safe was open, but I waited for Sister Jeanette to put the ledgers in. Maybe *she* threw Mother Celeste over the railing. She's old, but she's strong. She had a motive. How would it feel to have cancer and not be allowed to get good treatment? Especially if you were a nurse and knew incompetence when you saw it. Mother Celeste was mean to everyone: Zita, Sharon, Jeanette, Barbara, even me. If I hadn't been in the car with Jack Braddock Saturday night, I would suspect myself.

Jeanette came back, and put the books in the safe. She closed the thick, black door, and twirled the dial so a robber wouldn't know the last number of the combination.

"Thank you, Sister," I said. "If Sharon is wondering where I went, will you please tell her I went uptown? I'll see her at four-thirty."

"Be good."

"Sister Jeanette?"

"Yes."

"Someone told me Mother Celeste was writing something Saturday night. Did you see her writing anything?"

"No. When?"

"At night. Was she writing something when you took Eddie Braddock in there?"

"No. I don't think so. I was in a hurry to get back to the meeting, though. I pushed him in there and went back. She could have been writing. She was sitting in her chair. She kept her prayerbooks on the table by that chair."

"Do you think I could see her prayerbooks?"

"I suppose so." Jeanette took me to Mother Celeste's room. The prayerbooks were on the nightstand. They were typical nun's prayerbooks, fat with holy cards, colored ribbons, third-class relics in crocheted covers. They were in good condition in spite of their age. Nuns handle their books with care. I looked through the missal, the breviary, the meditation books, the *Adelaide's Companion,* the *Prayerbook for Religious,* the *Holy Rule and Constitutions,* and books of devotions, novenas, and lives of saints. There were several notes in the books in Mother Celeste's handwriting. Some were reminders to herself about topics for articles. Some were lists of things to do. Most had old creases. There was nothing that looked as if it had been written Saturday.

Sister Jeanette looked through the books, too. "There's nothing here, Frances," she said. "When I cleaned in here Sunday, I would have found anything she wrote.''

''Was there anything in the wastebasket when you cleaned?''

''Nothing.''

''You're sure?''

''Positive. I dispose of stuff from these trash cans very carefully. That's nurse's training. I would have noticed.''

''Where is the stationery?''

''Here, in her drawer.'' Jeanette opened the top drawer in the bedside stand. There was a box of stationery and envelopes. There were a few pens and pencils.

I looked through the stationery. Nothing. ''Is everything here in this room that was here before Mother Celeste died?''

''Everything. Well, I've changed the sheets, of course. Everything else is the same.''

''Could she have mailed a letter?''

''No. There were no letters in the office out-box Sunday morning. And she would have given it to me, anyway.''

''She could have given it to one of the Rosses.''

''That's true.''

''Nothing else was in the room?''

''Well, her habit was in here.''

''Her habit?''

''The habit she's wearing now. Mother had me get everything ready a month ago. She knew she was going to die, and she wanted to be buried in the old habit. Most of the old nuns have saved a habit to be buried in. Me, too. When we stopped wearing the old habit, most of us saved one. Mother had me pack her habit in a box. Folded just so. Tied with ribbons. Folded just the way our habits were when the bishop gave them to us at reception. Mother had me put the habit in and everything else. She had saved a headband that fit her well, and a guimpe, and a coif. Everything. She had me wash everything, and starch it, and iron it. She checked on every detail. Mother put her cincture in the box, herself. And her veil. Her rosary. Her vows. A petticoat, stockings. She kept the box right there on that step-stool by the bed. She was always reaching in it, making sure everything was just so. I took the box with me to Braddock Brothers Sunday morning. After all the checking, we still forgot a liner. That's why we had to call Sister Zita to bring a liner. Mother had even thought to have me take the medals off her rosary because they were silver. She had already taken off her profession ring. She didn't want to be buried with anything valuable. She thought of everything.''

I went back to the rotunda. A few visitors were standing around the book, examining the signatures and sentiments. I looked in the chapel. A few people were kneeling in the pews. A few were standing around the casket, looking at Mother Celeste's body.

TWENTY-SIX

I GOT IN MY CAR, phoned for messages, made some phone calls, and loaded my gun. As I drove uptown, I tapped the little tape recorder in my pocket and recorded my thoughts about the case. I parked on the square in front of the funeral home. Jack Braddock came outside. "Have you had lunch?"

"Not yet."

"I'm on my way to Harley's. Join me?"

We walked around the square. As we passed the feed store, I said, "Let's go in."

The fragrance in the dark, dusty interior of the store was intoxicating. We walked among the bags and barrels, touched the seed and feed, sifted it through our fingers. When we went back outside, we saw Pauline coming out of the *Herald* office.

"Did you recover?" Pauline asked me.

"I slept till eleven," I said.

"How's the paper selling?" Jack asked. "You want me to stand out here and yell, 'Extry, extry?'"

"Everybody's coming in to congratulate me," Pauline said. "I think I'll probably get a Pulitzer."

"You should," I said.

"Had lunch?" Jack asked.

"No, but I can't now. My mother's giving a party for the bishop tonight, and I've got to get over there and help her get ready."

In Harley's, several people were reading the special edition. We sat in a back booth. After we ordered, I said, "What did you and your brother mean last night about your grandmother and Mother Celeste?"

"They were both in love with Henry Braddock. Henry was a gay blade in his day. Old sense of the word. They both wanted to marry him. And every other girl in town, according to Grandma. Grandma used to say he wrote letters to both of them from Harvard. Stella and Celeste. Stringing them along. But Stella always knew he would marry her. And when he proposed to Stella, Celeste threw a fit. She was afraid she'd be left to marry a farmer, a clodhopper. Henry was the only game in town, and Stella won. Celeste was always jealous of Stella, to hear Stella tell it. Jealous, period. That's why she entered the convent. She didn't want to be less important than her sister. Stella would be the wife of the banker, the leading lady in the town. So Celeste decided she'd be a nun. Mother superior. She set her sights on that from the start, and she got what she wanted."

Jack picked up a copy of the *Herald* that someone had left in the booth. We looked at Henry Braddock. "He looks exactly like Eddie," I said.

"Grandpa was a weak man," Jack said. "And Eddie's weak, too."

Our food came. After a few minutes, I asked, "What was it like growing up in a funeral home?"

"It was okay. My mom fixed up the upstairs like an apartment. We never used the downstairs. We used the kitchen, but our living room and bedrooms were upstairs. You don't pay any attention to the fact that there might be a dead body or two downstairs. It isn't scary. It's nature. Death is part of life."

"I could see you at your desk from the Rosses' porch the other night."

"That's my room. I'd like to show it to you. Want to see it?"

"Sure."

It was getting cloudy again as we left the drugstore. We passed the bank, and Jack tapped on Eddie's window and waved.

There were no dead bodies in the funeral home. Al Braddock was sitting at the kitchen table with two old women. He introduced us. They were relatives who had come for the funeral.

Jack took me upstairs. The second floor of the big house was divided down the middle by a hall that surrounded the stairway. Each brother had a side for his own use. Jack's side had a sitting room, a bedroom, a bathroom, and a guest room. His rooms were beautifully furnished with leather arm chairs and mission tables. The floors gleamed. His bedroom was in the front corner of the house. One side faced the Rosses' house across the street, and the other side faced the square. In the corner of the room was a circular staircase. "Would you like to see the tower?"

"Yes."

Jack went up first. He had to raise a trap door at the top of the staircase and climb through it. "Okay, come up. Be careful."

He helped me step from the circular staircase into the little room. Then, he lowered the door. The tower room was about eight feet square, and surrounded by windows. There was a roll-top desk in the room, two glass-fronted bookshelves, and a wooden swivel chair.

"This was Grandpa's home office," Jack said. "After he and Grandma and Eddie moved out to the farm, my parents just left it like it was. The bedroom below was their bedroom, and they never used this room. After my mom died, I used to come up here and hide. Now, I still keep it like it was. It's not a shrine or anything. I just leave it alone. My kids come up here sometimes and play office.''

TWENTY-SEVEN

I DROVE BACK out to St. Adelaide's. Up in the dorm, Zita had posted the schedule on the bulletin board. Vespers at five. Supper at six o'clock in the girls' dining room for everybody. Hierarchy, clergy, religious, and guests would sup together. Vigil service at seven-thirty. Get-together for guests in the alumnae room after the service. On Wednesday morning, breakfast would be served from seven until eight for guests in the dining room. The funeral mass would be at ten. Following the burial, a buffet luncheon would be served in the girls' dining room, hosted by Al and Jack Braddock.

I went to my room to think. I climbed out on the fire escape and watched the scene below. The old nuns in their wheelchairs on the convent porch were fanning. The air was still and stifling.

The storm came suddenly. A bolt of lightning was followed by rumbling thunder that seemed to go on forever. People scurried for shelter. I jumped inside. Hail began to fall. Within a few minutes, the campus was covered with marble-sized hailstones. July had turned to December. I reached out my window and got a handful of hailstones from the fire escape. The rain came down in torrents.

I went through the tunnel to the motherhouse. In the alumnae room, women were playing bridge. In the chapel, visitors were praying by Mother Celeste's coffin, and an old nun was making the stations of the cross in her wheelchair.

Sharon was in the office. "Let's go in Mother's office," she said.

Mother Celeste's office was across the hall. The room was long and narrow. One end was furnished like a sitting room, and the other end like an office. Sharon closed the door and flopped down on a sofa.

"Are you okay?" I asked.

"The bishop wants to know what's going on."

"About what?"

"About everything. He's had calls from people complaining about money. We have unpaid bills. He wants to know what's going on. He's even had a call about you."

"About me?"

"Eddie Braddock."

"Called the bishop?"

"This morning."

I felt a little nervous. An atavistic fear took hold of me. What could the bishop do to me? Burn me at the stake? Excommunicate me? "What about?"

"He told him that Jack and Al, his good-for-nothing nephews, had brought in a private investigator, a woman, to snoop into his business and his aunt's business and the Church's business. You're damaging the Church's reputation. Eddie's also mad about not being told that I was acting superior. Et cetera."

"So what's the bishop going to do?"

"Nothing yet. Respect for the dead. Get Mother Celeste buried first, and then we'll get down to the nitty-gritty. He wants to see me again tomorrow at two. He wants to see you, too."

"What's the worst he can do to you?"

"Throw us out on the street. Take the buildings and the land. Put the old nuns in a nursing home."

"He could do that?"

"Bishops have been doing stuff like that to nuns for centuries."

"He's not going to do that. There's a real estate depression on. He couldn't sell this place if his life depended on it. Isn't it in the community's name?"

"Bishops can do anything they want. Who's going to stop him?"

It was very depressing. Outside, the rain poured down. Inside, my friend was collapsed on a sofa, almost in tears. I walked around the big office, looking at the books on the shelves, the degrees and awards on the walls, the prie-dieu in front of a big crucifix.

At five minutes to five, we heard the wooden clacker sounding in the rotunda. Sharon locked Mother Celeste's office, and we went into the chapel.

The bishop and his men were in the sanctuary. They were in cassocks and surplices, ready to preside over vespers. The chapel was filled with nuns and guests. Jack and Al and Eddie and the two old women were kneeling in the front pew by Mother Celeste's coffin. I went up the side aisle and found a place in the choir chapel. There was a folder in each stall with the evening prayer from the office of the dead.

The bishop intoned the office, and the congregation took it up. Everyone prayed enthusiastically, and it went well. The psalmody was accompanied by thunder and lightning. "Out of the depths, I cry unto you, O Lord," we sang, and lightning illuminated the stained-glass windows.

After the service, people stood around in the rotunda or went to the alumnae room to wait for supper. Jack and I slipped outside. The rain was slowing down. We drove uptown in Jack's car.

The dining room at the Southern Hotel was crowded, but Jack knew the waiter, and we got a corner table by the window. Across the square, the two big houses looked purple through the soft drizzle. "I envy you," I said. "It's so beautiful here. It's like living in an impressionist painting."

"You brought the weather with you. Usually it would be about a hundred this time of year, and the grass would be a nice, crispy brown."

"It's so beautiful."

"It *is* nice. You should come down more often. It's nothing to drive."

The waiter brought our drinks. Jack asked me if I had reached any conclusions yet. A group of priests was sitting at the next table, so we spoke softly. I told Jack about the suicide notes, the convent's financial state, and the missing piece of paper that Mother Celeste was seen writing on.

"Someone was in your room?"

"Yes. Sunday afternoon when I went to Kansas City."

"Why didn't you tell me that before?"

"I don't know."

"Are you sure?"

"Yes." I told him about the wardrobe door I never closed tightly and the blotter in the desk drawer.

At seven, Jack drove me back to the old convent and dropped me off. He had to make a phone call before the vigil service, he said.

At seven-thirty, everyone was back in chapel. Sister Sharon conducted the vigil service. Various nuns, alumnae, relatives, and friends went up to the sanctuary steps to read little poems or paragraphs or prayers they had written. The nuns sang a couple of hymns Mother Celeste had liked. Sharon read a passage from *Walsh's Creek.*

After the service, I sat still for a few minutes waiting for the chapel to clear out. When I went out to the rotunda, I saw the bishop talking to Peter Ross, the only Knight of the Holy Sepulcher in Braddock. Winnie Ross, wearing the only Chanel suit in Braddock, came over to me. "Frances," she said, "you're coming, aren't you?"

Pauline, Jack, and Al came across the rotunda. "I'll bring her, Mom," Pauline said.

"And Jack and Al, of course. You're coming, aren't you?"

"Yes, Ma'am," Al said.

Eddie Braddock was by the visitors' book, making sure everyone had signed. A group of women was heading for the party in the alumnae room. The nuns would not be attending either party.

Sharon walked us to the door.

The rain had stopped, and the sky was clearing. The sun was setting behind massive purple and orange clouds.

"Whose car?" Jack asked.

"Mine," Pauline said.

Jack drove. "Shall I go the long way?" He drove out to the roadhouse. It was nearly empty, and the band had not arrived yet. We danced for a while to music from the jukebox.

At ten, we went back to town. Jack parked Pauline's car in the funeral home parking lot, and we walked across the street to the Rosses' house. A group of priests sat on the porch. We went inside, and Winnie led us into the library where the bishop was holding court. Peter Ross was there along with the bishop's three assistants. On the wall was a large picture of Peter and Winnie Ross with Pius XII.

Winnie introduced Pauline first. "May I present my daughter Pauline, Your Excellency?"

The bishop held out his hand, and Pauline kissed his ring.

"My daughter's friend, Ms. Frances Finn, Your Excellency."

I shook his hand. My dad taught me long ago that Americans don't kiss people's rings.

"Mother Celeste's dear nephews and our favorite neighbors, Mr. Alcott Braddock and Mr. John Braddock."

Al kissed the bishop's ring, and Jack shook his hand. The bishop expressed his sympathy to them for their loss of their great-aunt. He congratulated Pauline on the special edition of the *Herald*.

We left the library as Winnie ushered in another set of guests. In the dining room, the Rosses' cook, Connie Cruz, was presiding over the buffet. Her husband, Rudy, was mixing drinks.

"What would you like to drink?" Rudy asked.

"Whatever the bishop's having," Jack said.

"He's on his third martini."

"Martini's good."

"Same for me," Pauline said.

"Frances?"

"Coke. Thank you."

"Rum and Coke," Al said.

Tom Ross and the priests who were staying at his house came into the dining room. They filled their plates from the elaborate chafing dishes, and went into the living room.

Winnie came into the dining room to look things

over. "Nice party, Mom," Pauline said. "A real old-fashioned, Irish wake."

"Thank you, dear. Mingle. Talk to the bishop."

Pauline and Al went back into the library. Jack and I went into the living room. Jack resumed a conversation about sports with a priest he had been talking to the night before.

I said to Tom, "I wonder if I could have a word with you in private."

"Sure. Let's go upstairs." We went into a sitting room on the second floor of the Rosses' house and sat down. "What's on your mind?"

"I'm investigating the circumstances surrounding Mother Celeste's death. I don't know if you've heard."

"I've heard."

"You were the last one to see her Saturday night."

"I guess I was."

"Did you see her writing something?"

"I didn't see her writing, but I could see that she had been writing. On her table she had a piece of paper and a pen."

"Could you see what was written on it?"

"No. I didn't try to, though."

"What did you talk about?"

"The obvious thing. Barbara's note."

"I read your note from Barbara."

"How? When?"

"At your house. Last night. I went in your room, and read it."

"It doesn't matter."

"What does Mitoo mean? And Witoo?"

"Twin language. Barbara and I had our own language when we were babies. It's hard to explain. It's a consonant language. Baby talk. Some words have more than one meaning. Mitoo meant something like, my two, my twin, my other. Mitoo. We called each other that. It was our name for each other.''

"And Witoo?''

"With you, more or less. It meant, we two, or with you. It meant, we are two, combined. We two do everything together. If one can't finish something, the other one will.''

"What did your sister mean by it in her letter?''

"I don't know. If I had gotten the letter when she wrote it, I would have taken it to mean, get revenge. Finish this matter for me. This thing I can't finish. Or maybe, we two must be together. Follow me. Kill yourself.''

"Would you have killed yourself if Barbara told you to?''

"I don't know. I can't really remember how I was then. So much time has passed. We were kids. Now, so much time has passed, and I've heard so many sad stories, that our little tragedy of not having the guts to stand up to our dad seems pitiful.'' This man who had stood in his yard raving about Sharon being a murderer three days earlier was now talking like a human being.

"Why didn't you just leave if you were so unhappy? You and Barbara.''

"We talked about it. Before Barbara made final vows, before I was ordained, we talked about it. We had a plan. We were going to run away together. To Canada. We were going to live in Toronto. I don't know how Barbara came up with that idea. We talked about it, but when it came down to really doing it, it was a childish fantasy. We couldn't do it. I could have saved my sister's life if I hadn't been such a fool. Such a coward. That's what I live with every day. We could have just walked away. We were adults. We could have gotten jobs. We could have gone to school, had careers, had relationships, gotten married, had kids, led normal lives. I can't explain why we didn't do it. What fear held us. Fear of our dad and the Church.''

''Why did you think Sharon had something to do with Barbara's death?''

''I guess I always connected her with that summer when we were home. That's when Barbara and I planned to run away to Canada. Sharon was there, staying at our house. I didn't have the courage to run away, so for some reason, I tried to blame Sharon. I can't explain it. For years I blocked out that summer. I told myself it wasn't my fault or Barbara's fault. It wasn't my parents' fault. But it had to be somebody's fault. The disaster. The death of my twin sister was a result of that summer. After that summer, we kind of gave up. I guess I focused my failure on Sharon. It doesn't make sense. She's so normal. I guess I hated her for being normal. It was easier to pretend that someone else was to blame for what happened than to accept the blame myself.''

''Sister Jeanette told me you used to go out at night and talk to Mother Celeste.''

''Yes. Two lonely people. Too educated to talk to the townsfolk. We talked about books. Never about Barbara.''

''What did Mother Celeste say to you Saturday night? Did you hear her confession?''

''She told me she wanted to talk to me first. No seal of confession. She told me she wanted to talk about Barbara. She said she was sorry for the way she had treated Barbara. She said she had made a lot of mistakes in her life, but that was the worst. Then she said she wanted to confess.''

''I guess you can't tell me what she said.''

''I couldn't if she had said anything specific, but she

didn't. It was very general. A typical nun's confession. I gave her absolution. I left.''

''How did you leave?''

''I left by the door in her room. I pulled it closed. Like I always did. Out to the porch. My car was parked out in front. I sat in my car for a few minutes. Trying to calm down.''

''You were perturbed?''

''Obviously.''

''You didn't see anyone else go in?''

''No one else was around. My car was the last one there. I guess the nuns' cars were there somewhere, but mine was the only one in front.''

''What time was it when you left?''

''I left Mother Celeste's room at ten.''

''She didn't give you a letter to mail?''

''No.'' He sat there with his big hands on his big knees. Had he thrown Mother Celeste off the convent porch? He was big enough. He had a motive. Witoo. We two work together. Get revenge. But he was too calm.

''Well, thank you for answering my questions. Do you have any idea of who might have gone into Mother Celeste's room later?''

''No. Are you certain somebody did?''

''Pretty certain.''

''What about Randy Hermann? Does he agree with you?''

''I don't know.''

We went back downstairs.

Jack took my hand, and led me through the kitchen to the back garden. ''Having fun?''

''No.'' The moonflowers on the garden fence were open to the night, and their fragrance brought tears to my eyes. My mother had loved the moonflower vine that grew on our garage when I was very young.

We stood by the flowers gleaming white in the darkness. Suddenly, an idea came to me. "Jack, will you drive me back to St. Ad's?"

"Sure. Getting tired?"

"I just thought of a place to look for whatever it was Mother Celeste was writing."

"I'll go in and give Pauline her keys. We'll take my car."

Jack went inside, and I walked across the street to the funeral home.

He came outside and crossed the street. "I'll be right back," he said. "I'll get my car keys." He went in the kitchen door. In a couple of minutes, he came back outside. We got in one of the Cadillacs and drove out to St. Adelaide's. "What's your idea?" he asked.

"It just popped into my head." I told him where I planned to look.

We parked on the grass in front of the motherhouse. We went up the steps. The front door was still open. The party in the alumnae room was still going on. We walked across the rotunda. The doors to the chapel were closed.

I pushed one of the doors open, and we went in. The chapel was nearly dark. The six candles burned around the catafalque, and the sanctuary lamp burned red by the altar.

We walked up the aisle. At the coffin, I stopped and looked down at Mother Celeste. Then, I took the rolled piece of paper from her hands.

TWENTY-EIGHT

I LED JACK through the choir chapel and into the priests' sacristy. I turned on the light. I removed the white ribbon and unrolled the piece of parchment. Another piece of paper was rolled inside it. On the parchment, a young nun had written her vows seventy-five years earlier. On the stationery, an old superior had written her last words to her community.

Dearest Sisters,

I have been an unworthy steward. From the day I took office, I used the community's money to support my cousin, Henry Braddock, in his banking business. The bank had its ups and downs, mostly downs, and Henry turned to me again and again. Now, at the end of my life, I have decided to tell you the truth so as not to leave you orphans.

All my life I prayed for the grace of final repentance, and that grace has been granted me. I am truly sorry. I will confess my sins to Father Ross tonight, and I confess my sins to you with this letter.

I lent the founders' patrimonies to Henry in 1933. He had tried to borrow money from them, but they refused. He had explained to them that without the money in the community's account, the bank would fail. Without the bank, the town and the farmers would fail. When I took office, I decided to help him. Henry intended to pay the money back, but the depression got worse. I let him use the money in the interest-bearing accounts, the nuns' dowries. When sisters' parents died, I lent the inheritances to Henry Braddock. There were other loans over the years: money from tuition, from my book, from the sale of cattle and hogs, and from memorial gifts from alumnae.

Sister Barbara's dowry paid for the juniorate. The memorial fund set up by the Ross family paid back the dowries to the sisters who left after Vatican II.

I lent the money from the highway commission and from the antique sale to my nephew, Edgar Braddock. The receipts and I.O.U.s from all the transactions are in order. They exist in duplicate. Henry Braddock kept one copy of each, and I kept the other. Later, Edgar Braddock kept copies of the receipts for funds I lent him. My copies of all the receipts for community funds lent to the Bank of Braddock are in my trunk.

Forgive me, Sisters. Pray for the poor soul of

Celeste, R.S.A.

Jack and I looked at each other. He spoke first. "I know where Henry's copies are."

"Where?"

"Up in the tower. Grandpa had some old ledgers in his bookshelves up there. There were loose papers in them. Some of them were on St. Adelaide's stationery. Some on bank paper. I remember seeing them when I was a kid."

The door opened then. Eddie Braddock stepped from the dark choir chapel into the sacristy. He had a gun in his hand. He pointed it at us. "Put the papers on the table."

"You gonna shoot us, Eddie?" Jack said.

"Shut up, Jack." Eddie's voice was low and deadly.

"Eddie, what's the deal? Are you nuts?"

"Shut up, Jack. Just shut up."

I put the two papers on the vestment case. My loaded gun was in my shoulder bag. If I could get it out, I would kill Eddie Braddock with pleasure. My loaded tape recorder was in the pocket of my jacket. If I could tap it, it would start recording.

Eddie picked up the papers. He glanced at Mother Celeste's formula of vows and tossed it aside. He studied the letter, keeping his gun pointed at us. "Okay," he said. "Next stop, the trunk room. Lead the way, Ms. Finn."

I started for the door to the choir chapel, but Eddie pointed to the back door with his gun. "Down the steps." There was a stairway leading down from the priests' sacristy to a back door of the motherhouse. This provided a way for the chaplain to get from his house to the chapel without going all the way around to the front of the building.

On the ground floor, instead of going outside, Eddie pointed with his gun to another door, this one to the nuns' refectory. We walked through the refectory. The light on the garage door outside shone through the windows of the big room.

We crossed the rotunda and went into the trunk room. In there, it was very dark. "Turn on the light, Ms. Finn," Eddie said.

"I don't know where it is," I said. My voice cracked with fear.

"Find it," Eddie said.

I pretended to feel the wall around the door as if I thought a light switch might be there. In my fumbling, I managed to tap my tape recorder through my pocket.

As his eyes adjusted to the darkness, Eddie said. "The string. Pull that string."

I pulled the string, turning on the dim light in the trunk room. Eddie closed the door to the rotunda.

"Now find my aunt's trunk."

I went to the nearest row of trunks, and bent down to examine the tags on them. I moved slowly, and read the tags with difficulty. I thought the longer I took, the better chance Jack and I would have to survive.

"Look back there. It's probably one of those old trunks."

I went back to the last row of trunks and crouched down to examine the tags.

"Why did you kill that poor old lady?" Jack asked.

"Shut up."

"You and Grandpa took money from the nuns to prop up the bank. All those years."

"Shut the fuck up, Jack."

"You gonna shoot me, Eddie? Go ahead. You can toss a dying old woman off a porch. Let's see if you can shoot a healthy young man."

"I'll shoot your girlfriend first."

"While you're shooting her, I'll climb up your ass and tear your head off."

I thought about dropping to the ground. Would I be able to get my gun out of my bag? Three rows of trunks were between Eddie and me. I kept crouching lower and lower to read the tags. It was nearly dark in the room. If he shot at me, he might miss. But he might not. He might shoot Jack first, and then take his time with me.

Would the people upstairs in the alumnae room hear the shots?

"You've got a big mouth, Jack. Just like your mother."

"And you've got a big gun. That makes you a big man. Just like your dad. Grandpa. Old Henry. Poor old Henry had to steal money from a bunch of nuns to keep his pathetic little bank going. And you're no better. How much have you taken, Eddie? I can make a guess about the highway part of it. 'Cause I know what I got."

"You shouldn't have gotten a nickel. My mother didn't intend for you to get a nickel. I told her not to break up the farm. But she always knew best. She thought it would be a joke to leave you that worthless bottom land."

"The joke was on you, wasn't it, Eddie?"

"She didn't intend for you and Al to get anything."

"Why was Grandma such a selfish old bitch, Eddie?"

"Shut up, Jack. My mother wasn't selfish."

I was moving slowly from trunk to trunk. If I could get my bag open, I would take out my gun, spin around, and blow Eddie's brains out.

"Then how come she left everything to you and nothing to my dad?"

"She knew Ollie was irresponsible."

"And you weren't? Then how come you needed to rob the nuns to keep the bank going?"

"Ollie didn't have sense enough to come in out of the rain."

"That's what he always said about you, Eddie."

"Mom and I weren't even sure you and Al were Ollie's kids. Ollie married trash. Your mother was trash, Jack. Did anyone ever tell you that? She was a lush. A drunk. Did you ever stop and think that you might not be a Braddock at all? Ollie was in Korea when you were conceived. My mom figured that out. Can you count to nine, Jack?''

"Where were you hiding, Eddie? How did you know where we were?''

"Shut up, Jack. I was in my aunt's room. I was looking in her stuff. I saw you and your girlfriend drive up. I watched you go in the chapel. I saw your girlfriend take the paper.''

"Where'd you get the gun, Eddie? I didn't know you carried a gun.''

"I went out and got it out of my car.''

I kept moving from trunk to trunk. I was feeling hot and dizzy. I knew I was going to faint if I didn't get some air, some relief from fear. I knew Eddie was going to kill us. He wouldn't be telling us his life story if he wasn't going to kill us. They would find the tape recorder in my pocket. They would know he did it. A lot of good that would do Jack and me. I hadn't taken this whole thing seriously. I was playing at investigating. Now Jack would die with me for my stupidity. And maybe others. Maybe Eddie would go upstairs after he killed us, and kill Sharon. He might kill everybody in the building.

"Hurry up," Eddie said in his murderous voice.

"You haven't answered my question," Jack said. "Why'd you kill Mother Celeste?''

"She was getting crazy. Out of control. She got your girlfriend down from Kansas City to pull a little trick on Sharon.''

"Why'd she do that, Eddie?''

"Sister Sharon was trying to get a look at the books. Mother Celeste figured she could keep Sharon away from the books if people thought she had killed Barbara. They might even think Sharon took the money. If Sharon would murder poor, sick Barbara Ross, why wouldn't she steal money?''

"So Mother Celeste was doing it to protect your sorry ass?''

"I guess so. I didn't ask her to do it. I didn't even know what she was up to till Saturday night. She told me what she had planned to do. That's when I knew she was out of control. The plan was crazy. Made no sense. When I found out Sharon had taken over the community, I knew my aunt was finished.''

"So you killed her. Real nice.''

"She told me she had decided to tell the nuns where the money went. She said she was going to write it down while her mind was clear. I couldn't let her do that. Whatever little money she lent the bank is history. There's nothing in any account that the convent could claim. I told her that. She said she was going to tell the nuns there were I.O.U.s. I couldn't let her do that. Not that any little scrap of paper from sixty years ago would have any legal standing today. All kinds of money disappeared back then. I told her to forget about it. I'd help her out if she had financial problems. But she had made up her mind to tell them.''

"She was gonna tell the nuns their money went down the toilet known as the Bank of Braddock?''

"She was sitting there with her glasses on, ready to write it all down. She wanted me to hand her a piece of stationery. I told her to forget it. I told her I'd go home, and look for the receipts, and I'd come back out later to talk about it.''

"Why didn't you just toss her over the railing then?''

"Shut up, Jack.'' To me, he said, "Hurry up.''

"So you came back later?"

"I walked across the field. After midnight."

"Was she happy to see you back, Eddie?"

"She wouldn't tell me what she did with the letter she wrote. I asked her if she wrote it, and she said yes. She was going to give it to Sharon in the morning. I couldn't let that happen."

"Is that when you threw her at the statue?"

"I told her I wanted the letter. That we'd explain to Sharon together. That I'd give Sharon the receipts, and explain. She wouldn't give me the letter. I tried to find it. I looked in her drawers and in her prayerbooks. She must have hid it in her vows when she heard me coming in the door. It took me a while to get the door open. It was raining so hard. I dropped the key. She must have rolled up that letter and stuck it in her vows. I didn't even think to look in that box. It was right there by her bed. It had been there for weeks. She had been talking about all the stuff in that box for weeks. Her habit. Her veil. The vows. I should have looked in the box."

"You couldn't find the letter, so you heaved her over the railing. You picked up a little old woman, nearly a hundred years old, and flung her against a concrete pedestal. Broke her bones. Cracked her skull. Way to go, Eddie."

I found Mother Celeste's trunk. I knew Eddie was going to kill us. He hadn't thought to take my bag. I had to take my gun out and shoot him.

"Is that it?" He saw that I had stopped.

"It's locked," I said.

"Leave it alone. Come back over here. Slow. Walk slow."

I went back to the center of the room.

"Now open that door." Eddie pointed to the door to one of the meat lockers.

I walked over to the heavy door. I turned the handle and pulled it open. A stale smell came from the dark locker. My legs were weak.

"Go in."

I was trying to keep from fainting. I was afraid if I fell, he'd shoot me on the floor. I stepped into the meat locker.

"You too, Jack."

"Horse shit, Eddie. Shoot me here."

"You think I won't?"

"You won't. If you were going to shoot me, you'd have shot me by now."

"Go in."

"I'm not going in there, Uncle Eddie. In that dark, scary meat locker? I could suffocate in there. I can't stand places like that. You're gonna have to shoot me first, Uncle Eddie. Then drag me in."

Inside the locker, I couldn't see. I put my hand in my pocket to make sure the tape recorder was still running. It was. I was afraid to move. I was afraid there were metal hooks on the wall. I was afraid Eddie would shoot us and hang us on metal hooks. Or just close the door on us and leave. We would suffocate in the meat locker. If we screamed, no one would hear us. No one would ever find us. The nuns hadn't used the meat lockers for years. Not since they sold the farm and the cows and the hogs. My brain was spinning out of control. No oxygen. Spinning. Spiraling down. From long experience with fainting, I knew that I had about five seconds left. I opened my bag, took out my gun, aimed for the ceiling of the meat locker, and somehow managed to pull the trigger.

As always, in a faint, I could still hear. The shot reverberated in the small metal and concrete room, re-sounded again and again, surrounded me with sound. It sounded like I had fired a hundred shots. I lay on my back. The heavy Smith and Wesson was still in my hand, but I had no strength. I couldn't open my eyes. My head felt like I had split it open on the concrete floor.

Someone was groaning. "No. No. You shot me." Staggering footsteps. Then Jack was beside me, holding my head.

"It's okay. Frances? Honey? Are you okay?"

"Where is he?"

"He won't get far. I shot him in the butt." Jack took the gun out of my hand. He helped me stand. He helped me out of the locker.

"You shot him?"

"I had my brother's gun in my pocket. I've been carrying it since Sunday. I figured if we were after a killer, I'd better be armed."

"You shot him?"

"I was just waiting for my chance. I knew he'd get distracted. You were perfect. Slow and cool. Taking your time. Our timing was perfect together. Like danc-ing. When you fired your gun in there, it sounded like a bomb went off. Eddie spun around, and I shot him in the butt."

"Where is he?" I staggered, and nearly fell again.

"He ran outside. He dropped his gun and grabbed his butt. He won't get far."

I got my purse and my gun from the floor of the meat locker. I could hear women running and yelling. "Call the police! A man has been shot! Get an ambulance!"

The women had run downstairs from the alumnae

room. Jack and I followed Eddie Braddock's trail of black blood to the south door. He was lying on his side on the ground just outside the door. A pool of blood was spreading on the driveway. Women were around him, trying to stanch the blood with handkerchiefs, trying to comfort him. He was screaming and cursing. The old nuns were leaning out their windows above.

Jack led me past Eddie.

Eddie saw us and screamed. "Call the police! That man tried to kill me. Jack Braddock!" The women shrank away from us.

Jack led me around to a bench in front of the motherhouse. He put his arms around me and held me until I stopped crying. Before I had stopped completely, the first cop car came roaring up the long drive, siren screaming, red light on top twirling.

Jack was holding me and talking to me. "You were great. Perfect. What a detective. You solved a murder. Congratulations. There's nothing to cry about. When you stepped into that meat locker, I knew we had him. Once we were separated, we were safe. He was never gonna get us both in there. Eddie's an idiot. He didn't even consider that we might have guns. Don't cry. Frances. Honey. We wouldn't have died in there even if he got us in there. There's a handle on the inside. Do you think they'd build a thing like a meat locker and not put a handle on the inside? Everything's okay. Here. Take this. It's clean. Blow your nose. You were perfect. Perfect timing. When you fired your gun in there, Eddie freaked out. I shot him right in the ass. I can't stand to shoot a quail, but I was ready to blow my uncle's head off. Something made me aim for his ass instead."

The second cop car came roaring in from the back gate. It squealed to a stop in front of us. Randy Hermann jumped out. Another cop, in uniform, with a huge flashlight, ran around to the south door.

"Jack?"

"Evening, Randy."

"What the fuck is going on here?"

"What I told you on the phone this evening?"

"Yeah?"

"Well, it looks like we were right."

Sister Zita and several women came running across the campus from the old convent. Zita was in her habit, and the women were in their pajamas and robes. Zita sat down beside me on the bench. "Are you all right?"

The chaplain and the order priests came running across the lilac field. Sharon and Jeanette came out on the porch and ran down the steps.

Another cop car and an ambulance came wailing up the long drive. I stood up. My head was throbbing, but I had to see. Jack and Zita and I walked around to the south door. Eddie Braddock was handcuffed now, still lying on the ground on his side. He was trying to use his hands to stop the blood still running from the bullet hole in his butt. He was cursing Randy Hermann. The red lights on the cop cars were spinning, and from the radios, the dispatcher's calm voice could be heard.

"Mr. Braddock," Chief Hermann was saying, "help me out, okay? Just take it easy. You're gonna be okay. An ambulance is on the way. I'm just trying to figure out what the fuck is going on."

TWENTY-NINE

THE NOISE of the women in the dorm woke me at seven.
It was like boarding school. Noise. I had had three hours
of sleep. The only thing missing was the sound of competing radios. The hot water heater had been turned on,
so I took a shower on the third floor. I could hear the
women at the sinks talking about the night before. The
town banker had murdered the mother superior. His
own aunt. Last night he tried to kill his own nephew. He
also tried to kill the woman who's in there taking a
shower.

I washed my hair carefully, trying to avoid the bump
on my head.

I went out on the fire escape. There were more cars
than ever on the campus. They were parked on the grass
all the way down to the pergola. It was perfect funeral
weather. There was a hearse parked on the sidewalk in
front of the motherhouse. Rudy Cruz was standing beside it.

I saw Jack and Al get out of one of the Cadillacs.
They were in their funeral suits. They went up the steps
to the motherhouse.

I got dressed in my own dark suit. I went down to
my car and called my answering machine. I drove uptown. I bought a *Kansas City Journal-Post* and went
into Harley's for bacon and eggs.

Back at St. Ad's, I went into the motherhouse to find
out what was going on. Sharon was in the office, wearing a navy blue dress. She came around from behind

the counter and put her arms around me. She had tears in her dark eyes. "It's unbelievable," she said. "You could have been killed."

I didn't want to think about it in this crowd of people. I didn't want to start shaking again. "What's going on?" I asked.

"The funeral mass is going to go on as planned," she said. "Randy Hermann told us to go ahead with that. But we'll have to wait a few days for the burial. Rudy Cruz will take Mother's body out to the hospital after the mass, and they'll do the autopsy there. We'll have a private burial in a couple of days."

"Where's Jack?"

"Down in the kitchen. Talking to the caterers."

"They're still having the luncheon?"

"People have to eat. The caterers came with their van at eight o'clock."

"Are you okay?" Last night at the police station, she had been pale and calm.

"I'm holding up. It's going to take a while to assimilate what happened."

Sister Jeanette came into the office. She was wearing a black suit. She gave me a hug, too. "You didn't know what you were getting into, did you?"

There were crowds of people in the halls and in the rotunda. Sharon said, "We'll talk later, okay?"

I walked around, looking at the people. There were nuns from other orders, priests, alumnae, people from the town, ex-nuns, relatives, friends, cops, even a reporter I knew from Kansas City. Rudy Cruz began tolling the old convent bell at quarter till ten. Everyone crowded into the chapel. Jack and Al and their relatives sat in the first pew. The nuns sat in the choir chapel.

Mother Celeste's coffin was closed now and covered with a black pall.

The nuns led the singing. Nearly everyone in the chapel remembered the words and the chant. The excitement over the events of the night before was audible in the enthusiastic singing. *Requiem aeternam dona eis, Domine.*

Zita and I stood in the back of the chapel by the confessional. A cop who had been at the police station the night before stood next to us. He had a beautiful, deep voice. *Et ab haedis me sequestra.*

The bishop preached a dramatic sermon that relied heavily on Pauline's chronology of Mother Celeste's life. He filled in the congregation on what the police procedure would be with Eddie Braddock. He was being held without bail. It was expected that he would plead guilty to murder since his confession had been taped by another of his intended victims. The bishop did not mention Mother Celeste's letter or the missing money. He reminded the people that a man is innocent until proven guilty. He asked them to pray for Eddie Braddock. He told them that Mother Celeste had been anointed in the hospital a few weeks before, and again, conditionally, on Sunday morning. She had confessed her sins the night before she died. She had made the Nine First Fridays again and again during her life and had received the grace of final repentance. Tom Ross was in the sanctuary with all the other priests.

At the end of the mass, the bishop circled the closed coffin, censed it, and sprinkled it with holy water. *Libera me, Domine, de morte aeterna.*

The organist played the introduction to the recessional. The nuns sang the hymn in English. Go forth to paradise, let angels take thee by the hand. Then, as Jack and Al wheeled the coffin to the door of the chapel, the bishop intoned the Miserere.

Six nuns carried the coffin down the steps to the hearse. Rudy Cruz stood at the open door and helped the pallbearers place the coffin in the hearse. Jack and Al closed the door. Everyone stood on the porch and on the steps. The priests and nuns recited the Miserere while the hearse moved slowly down the long drive. *Exultabunt Domino ossa humiliata.*

Mother Celeste had used the nuns' money to support her cousin's bank. For sixty years, she had given away the nuns' dowries, earnings, and inheritances to her relatives. The nuns ate rabbit while Mother Celeste's relatives lived in splendor. Mother Celeste has sacrificed a sick young nun to pay for a building. She had denied Zita an education and Jeanette medical care. She had tried to divert attention from the lost money by making wild accusations against Sharon. She had tried to use me for that. Who knew what else she had done?

THIRTY

AT THE FUNERAL feast, merriment was high. Everyone was thrilled to be alive. The hunger that follows a funeral had taken hold. Even the bishop was stuffing his face. The kitchen sisters were eating heartily, delighted to be partaking of food they hadn't cooked. Such expensive meats, such canapes, such dainty morsels had never been seen in this place. People shouted from table to table. The mother superior hadn't just died. She had been murdered. The killer was her own nephew, the town banker. Money is the root of all evil. People had come from far away for an exciting funeral. It had turned out to be even better than expected. People table hopped. Winnie Ross, elegant in black, wearing a hat that drew admiring glances from everyone in the room, came to my table. "Pauline told me what happened. It's unbelievable."

Jack was sitting at the next table with his red-haired daughters. He stood up to greet Winnie.

She kissed him. "How could this happen, Jack? Thank God you're all right."

Peter Ross and Sharon were at the bishop's table. The bishop was smiling at Sharon and patting her hand reassuringly between bites of lobster salad.

Jack and I walked down to the pergola after the luncheon. "What's going to happen?" I asked.

"Nothing for a long time. It'll take years to sort out. I'll keep you informed."

"What about Eddie?"

"He's already lining up lawyers."

"What about Sharon?"

"Sharon should turn this place into a retirement home. There's a retirement home for old ladies in Kansas City where I go to pick up a body every once in a while. The nuns up there tell me they have a thousand people on their waiting list. Sharon could fill this place up in a week. My cousins told me this morning they wish they could retire here. Beautiful campus. Peaceful. Safe. Safe, now that the village murderer is in jail. Sharon's got how many rooms here? A couple hundred? She could fill them in a week with paying customers. Not sick old ladies, but just old ladies that want a safe place to live. Chapel. Dining room. It's all here. Sharon could hire some women in town to cook and clean. Even nurses. My ex-wife is a nurse. She'd love to come out here and boss around a bunch of people. Sharon's got a gold mine here."

"You should advise her. You have a knack for making money."

"Al's got the knack, too. We'll help her. Don't worry. And we'll see what we can do to make the money reappear."

Clare CURZON

Monday was going to be a killer...

It's the worst day of the week for many people, but this particular Monday is brutal for Annette Briers. First, she finds out that her boss, Miranda Gregory, was the victim of a hit-and-run accident and is now hanging on for dear life. To make matters worse, she finds a dead stranger slumped over in her office chair.

As the police team tries to link the two crimes, they discover that the elegant Miranda Gregory is a mystery woman without a past, or so it seems. And it also becomes apparent that she holds the key to a secret that could lead to a murderer....

PAST MISCHIEF
A THAMES VALLEY MYSTERY

"...ingenious narrative...a true teaser."
—*New York Times Book Review*

Available in November 1997
at your favorite retail outlet.

WCC256

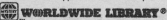